Praise for Lee Tob

"McClain pits her charming, au[...]
against the realistic problems o[...]
for a story that is deeply emotional but never soapy.
The welcoming community and beautifully described
scenery of Teaberry Island only enhance this cozy
romance. Readers won't want to put this down."
—*Publishers Weekly*, starred review,
on *The Forever Farmhouse*

"Lee Tobin McClain's books make my heart sing."
—Debbie Macomber, *New York Times* bestselling author

"Lee Tobin McClain dazzles with unforgettable
characters, fabulous small-town settings and a
big dose of heart. Her complex and satisfying stories
never disappoint."
—Susan Mallery, *New York Times* bestselling author

Praise for Kathryn Springer

"A feast of small-town charm and characters who feel
like dear friends."
—Liz Johnson, bestselling author of *The Red Door Inn*,
on *The Gathering Table*

"Heartwarmingly tender, wise and witty, with prose as
lush and delicious as chocolate ganache... I loved it!"
—Linda Goodnight, *New York Times* bestselling author
of *The Rain Sparrow*, on *The Gathering Table*

"A tender, touching story filled with memorable
characters who will sweep you away on a journey
of hope, second chances, and new beginnings.
Kathryn Springer skillfully blends multiple story lines
to create a rich, satisfying read."
—Irene Hannon, three-time RITA® Award winner,
on *The Gathering Table*

Lee Tobin McClain is the *New York Times* bestselling author of emotional small-town romances featuring flawed characters who find healing through friendship, faith and family. Lee grew up in Ohio and now lives in Western Pennsylvania, where she enjoys hiking with her goofy goldendoodle, visiting writer friends and admiring her daughter's mastery of the latest TikTok dances. Learn more about her books at www.leetobinmcclain.com.

USA TODAY bestselling author **Kathryn Springer** has written over thirty novels. She lives on a lake in northern Wisconsin and enjoys long walks in the woods and the change of seasons (although sometimes she wishes the "change" between winter and spring wouldn't last quite so long!). Kathryn loves to write stories that celebrate new beginnings and happily-ever-afters.

A Mother's Gift

LEE TOBIN McCLAIN
KATHRYN SPRINGER

LOVE INSPIRED
INSPIRATIONAL ROMANCE

LOVE INSPIRED®
INSPIRATIONAL ROMANCE

Recycling programs
for this product may
not exist in your area.

ISBN-13: 978-1-335-59878-3

A Mother's Gift

Copyright © 2024 by Harlequin Enterprises ULC

A Mother for His Child
Copyright © 2024 by Lee Tobin McClain

The Mommy List
Copyright © 2024 by Kathryn Springer

For questions and comments about the quality of this book, please contact us
at CustomerService@Harlequin.com.

® is a trademark of Harlequin Enterprises ULC.

Love Inspired
22 Adelaide St. West, 41st Floor
Toronto, Ontario M5H 4E3, Canada
www.LoveInspired.com

Printed in U.S.A.

CONTENTS

A MOTHER FOR HIS CHILD

Lee Tobin McClain

For mothers and caregivers everywhere.

For I know the thoughts that I think toward you, saith the Lord, thoughts of peace, and not of evil, to give you an expected end.
—*Jeremiah* 29:11

Chapter One

Blake Evans rushed into the Point diner, ignoring the rain dripping down his neck.

"Hi, Daddy." His five-year-old daughter, Wren, waved casually from a booth where she was sitting with a family he knew. She stuck a french fry in her mouth and went back to coloring beside her friend Zinnia.

Whew. Wren was fine.

He hung his coat on a hook, hugged his daughter and thanked his friends who were finishing their dinner and watching Wren. Then he approached Zoey Grey, who was wiping off the counter. And who'd been babysitting Wren, supposedly for the afternoon, only he'd been way late coming home. "I'm awful," he said to her. "I can't believe you had to bring her to work."

Zoey glared at him. "What else could I expect from an absent-minded professor?" Then her face broke into its usual smile.

Relieved, he smiled back. "You're the best, but... I'm still sorry. One of my first-year students was really struggling, and it turns out he has some problems at home, too, and so—"

She held up a hand. "Blake. It's fine. She's been playing with Zinnia for the past hour." She put her hands on the small of her back and stretched. "Let me guess. You're starving."

Blake's stomach chose that moment to let out a loud growl. "Yeah, but I'll fix something at home."

"I held back a blue plate special. Go talk to Wren, and I'll wrap it up."

His stomach growled again. "You shouldn't have, but thank you." Zoey was the best. She was so accepting, so kind. In the two years since his wife, Carol Ann, had died, Zoey had been an incredible support to him and Wren.

She was two years younger than him and had joined a large foster family near his parents' house when she was twelve. She'd struggled academically, and Carol Ann had tutored her throughout high school.

Blake had felt sorry for Zoey when he'd seen her being teased for her limited wardrobe soon after she'd arrived in town. He'd put the bullies in their place, and Carol Ann had given her some stylish clothes she didn't need anymore.

After Blake and Carol Ann had married, finished graduate school and returned to Holiday Point, they'd ended up living next door to Zoey's rented cottage. Their friendship had picked right back up where it had left off. Zoey had done a lot of babysitting for them as they'd started their busy careers as new professors. And once the aneurysm had taken Carol Ann, Zoey had stepped in to pick up the pieces and help Blake navigate single fatherhood. He didn't know what he and Wren would have done without her.

He went over and knelt beside Wren, hugging her to

his side. She was his world, and he needed to do better. Yes, she was totally safe and secure staying with Zoey, but he'd been wrong to be late.

"Look at my picture," she said and held up the coloring page. He admired it and then admired Zinnia's, too. "Thank you again for looking after her," he said to Alec and Kelly, Zinnia's parents. "I owe you. Next time you want a date night, Zinnia can come over and hang with us."

"You're on, man," Alec said with a fist bump. "But it's no problem. We're glad Zinnia and Wren have become friends. She's a great kid."

"She is." Blake smoothed back the hair that had escaped Wren's ponytail.

Zoey came out of the kitchen with a take-out container in her hands. A guy Blake didn't know, wearing a cook's apron, followed her out.

She was nodding. "Friday would work," she said.

Blake leaned over to see better. Who was this guy?

"Then it's a date," the cook said, smiling at Zoey.

Blake stood. Everything in him said *no*.

The guy leaned a hip against the counter and continued talking to Zoey.

Alec eased out of the booth and stood, blocking Blake's view of the annoying interaction. "Relax! The guy just fixed your dinner."

"What?" Blake refocused his attention onto his friend.

Alec nodded toward Zoey and the cook. "You looked like you were about to attack him with your butter knife."

"He's hitting on her." Blake craned around Alec to keep an eye on the man. If he tried anything...

"He's having a conversation with her."

Blake checked on Wren. She was talking a mile a minute to Alec's wife, Kelly, a teacher at the school where Wren attended kindergarten.

He stepped away from the table and looked down toward the kitchen. Zoey and the cook were still talking. The cook said something that made Zoey laugh. Then he touched her arm.

Blake's jaw clenched.

Alec stepped to the side, blocking his view again. "She's single, pretty and nice. Why wouldn't he want to talk to her?"

"Yeah, but..." Blake didn't know what he wanted to say.

"But what?" Alec studied him, eyebrows raised.

"Can't I look out for my friend? He's not good enough for her."

Alec beckoned him toward the counter, out of earshot of the girls. "Why don't *you* ask her out?"

Blake stared. "Me? I couldn't. I'm still... It hasn't been that long." And there was no way Zoey would go out with someone like him, older and nerdy and already a father.

"Two years since Carol Ann passed, right? And you're not getting any younger."

"No way." The thought of asking Zoey out made him extremely uncomfortable. Because what if she said no and it affected their friendship? He couldn't get by without Zoey. Not just because of how wonderful she was with Wren, but because…well. Knowing Zoey was nearby just made things right with the world. Everyone needed a friend like Zoey. He was blessed to have her, and he couldn't put that into jeopardy.

Besides, he'd been inferior as a husband. He knew that without a doubt. So there was no way he'd inflict himself on a wonderful woman like Zoey. He'd learned from his mistakes.

Alec shrugged. "Your loss," he said. His wife, Kelly, slid out of the booth. Zinnia and Wren hugged each other goodbye. Alec helped Kelly and Zinnia into their jackets, and the little family left, Alec with his arm protectively around Kelly.

The sight gave Blake a little pang near his heart. Was he ever going to put his arm around someone again?

Wren reached up, and Blake sat on the edge of the booth they'd just vacated and pulled her into his lap.

She stuck her thumb in her mouth and leaned against his chest. He started to tell her not to suck her thumb, but then stopped and just held her close, stroking her hair.

Wren was fine so much of the time, but a few little habits like the thumb sucking revealed she was still having trouble with the loss of her mom. People had warned him about future orthodontia bills, and he was trying to help her kick the habit. But sometimes, he gave in to the urge to simply comfort her.

Wren was his focus, had to be.

He couldn't think about the longings that sometimes came to him, the loneliness.

Everyone had problems. His biggest one had been losing his wife.

So he hadn't had the best marriage, hadn't been the best husband. There was no need to pity himself about that.

That cook was *still* chatting up Zoey.

He stood, lifting Wren with him and perching her on his hip. He walked over. "I'll take you home whenever you're ready, Zoey," he said.

Both the cook and Zoey looked startled. So maybe he'd spoken a little too aggressively.

"I'm on the clock for another half hour," Zoey said. "You don't have to wait. I can walk home."

"Or I can drive you," the cook said hopefully. "It's raining out."

"It's no problem," Blake barked. "I'll get her home."

"If you're sure. Thanks, Blake. I'd better check on my customers." She eased her way out from in between the two of them and grabbed a coffeepot from behind the counter.

"We're on for Friday, right?" the cook called after Zoey.

"Yes! Sure. See you then."

Blake's gut twisted. He'd always had a protective, big-brother feeling toward Zoey. That was what this was all about. Wasn't it?

He had no right to do it, but he drew himself up and glared at the guy, who was several inches shorter and several years younger than he was. He didn't stop until the man went back into the kitchen.

He wanted to make sure the guy knew that Zoey

wasn't on her own, that she had a friend in her corner if someone she dated did even one thing she didn't like.

Surely Zoey had imagined the awkwardness of that encounter. Blake had glared after Larry the cook and then stood close by her, as if he were her big brother. Or...as if he felt possessive of her. Which was ridiculous.

She'd spent plenty of time imagining him looking at her in some kind of a way. Really, ever since he and Carol Ann had saved her from a group of kids jeering at her in middle school.

But the way he'd stepped in just now and insisted on driving her home meant nothing. Or at most, it was gratitude toward her for going the extra mile caring for Wren.

More likely, he was thinking about some important equation. Blake was known in town—indeed nationally—for his smarts. The polar opposite of Zoey, who'd struggled in school.

Blake had sat down in one of the chairs by the door, holding a sleepy Wren.

"I have to get checks to a couple of my customers, and then I'll be ready to go," she told him.

"Before you go, can you help me fix this cash register?" At the other end of the counter, Rena Owen, who owned the diner, was punching buttons to no avail. "I'm getting us a new register ASAP."

"Sure." Zoey walked across the diner, studied the

ancient machine then grabbed a knife and pried open the side panel.

"I didn't know Blake was a relative of yours," Rena said.

Zoey gently slid the knife in and eased out a wrinkled piece of register tape. "He's not. We're just friends."

"How'd you get into caring for his kid?" Rena asked, her voice low enough that Blake, across the diner, couldn't hear. She was relatively new in town and didn't know the history.

Zoey explained about Carol Ann. "She got me through school, and when they had a child, I was a natural to babysit." She rewound the remaining tape and closed the machine.

"Any romantic interest between you now?"

"No!" Zoey punched the buttons for the final readout. "No way. He's out of my league."

"Wait, there are leagues?" Rena deadpanned. She patted the cash register and smiled at Zoey. "Thank you! You're a genius."

"Right. I'm the girl who had to take basic algebra twice." Zoey leaned a hip against the counter. "Are you planning to date in Holiday Point?"

Rena waved a hand. "Nope. Been there, done that. I'm here to run my business." She pointed a menu at Zoey. "But you, you should date. If not him, someone else."

"I have a date Friday night," Zoey said.

The words felt funny coming out of her mouth. She hadn't dated much in the past few years. Too busy working, picking up all the extra shifts she could, trying to get her credit cards paid off. She'd like to get a better car, too.

Plus, the guys in this town weren't what she was looking for. Try as she might, she couldn't see a bowling date as romantic.

She glanced at Blake, then away.

"Who's your date?" Rena asked.

"Larry. Our cook."

Rena tilted her head. "Funny, I wouldn't have thought he was your type."

"I don't *have* a type. But I'm trying to find one." She sighed. "I'm not getting any younger. I'd like to start a family."

But at the age of twenty-nine, she needed to get cracking. She needed to build a relationship with a nice guy, and to do that, you had to date. Had to give all different types of guys a chance.

When Zoey headed over to where Wren and Blake sat, Wren jumped up and grabbed her hand, then turned back to Blake. "Daddy, can I ask her now?"

"Wren, we just discussed—"

"Can you come to Muffins with Mom this week?" Wren took her other hand and danced back and forth. "I need a mommy to come."

"Wren, honey," Blake said with an apologetic look at Zoey. "You'll have *two* grandmas there."

"But I want a mommy."

"When is it?" Zoey asked. Wren was so cute.

"It's this Thursday morning at the elementary school," Blake said. "A Mother's Day event. Some of the dads get together and cook breakfast for the moms. Or mother figures. Which Wren has in her grandmothers."

Zoey felt a pang. Mother's Day wasn't a favorite with her.

She'd never had a mom to bring to school events like that. When she was small, her biological family had moved from place to place too rapidly to figure out and participate in school events, not that her parents would have wanted to. After they'd lost custody and she'd been placed in foster care, it had mostly been in bigger families where mothers were spread thin. By the time she'd moved to Holiday Point, she'd stopped asking her foster parents to come to anything.

Now, as an adult, she felt sad not to have a child to love on Mother's Day. Having kids was all she'd ever wanted to do, but prospects were not good for her here in Holiday Point. She might never have a child of her own to invite her to Muffins with Mom.

Then again, she'd just been invited by a child she adored. She looked at Blake.

His forehead wrinkled. "You don't have to do it."

"Please, please, please come," Wren begged.

"She's probably busy, honey," Blake said. Quietly, he added, "It's fine. Don't worry about it," to Zoey.

Wren looked crushed. Her slumped shoulders reminded Zoey of how she'd felt so many Mother's Days in her life. "I can come, honey," Zoey said, hugging her. "I'm already looking forward to our special time together."

Chapter Two

Muffins with Mom. A bittersweet event.

This morning, Blake had found a photo of Wren and Carol Ann on an earlier Mother's Day, when she was two and they'd gone to Carol Ann's parents to celebrate. He'd sat down with Wren and talked about the day, how she and Carol Ann had worn matching outfits.

That was what psychologists said to do—don't make the loss a secret, talk about it, show children that it was okay to be sad and miss people who had gone out of their lives.

Now, he deposited Wren with her two doting—and sometimes dueling—grandmothers in the elementary school cafeteria and headed back into the kitchen to help prepare breakfast.

Maybe Zoey wouldn't come. Blake couldn't hope for that, not when it would be so disappointing to Wren. But for himself, he'd just as soon she didn't. He'd been fighting off strange feelings ever since he'd learned Zoey was going out on a date.

Had she ever gone on a date before? Not lately, he was pretty sure.

He couldn't imagine why not, and yet…he liked that she didn't date. If she had a boyfriend, it would change their friendship.

"Controlled chaos back here." One of the other

dads, Cam Wilkins, handed Blake an apron. "You want to break about four dozen eggs for me?"

"Sure thing." Blake was a half-decent breakfast cook. Lunch, too, for that matter. It was dinner he had trouble with. That was why he and Wren ended up eating so much pizza.

And so many meals at the diner. With Zoey.

He looked out the pass-through window into the cafeteria. Wren was where he'd left her, talking with her two grandmas. And...uh-oh.

Zoey was approaching the table, and Wren jumped off his mother's lap and ran to her. She tugged Zoey toward the table, chattering up a storm.

Too late, he realized he should have let the grandmas know that Zoey was coming.

Blake couldn't hear what was being said, but he could read body language. His mother smiled and greeted Zoey, but Carol Ann's mother stiffened. The way Wren was hanging on Zoey didn't improve the situation.

He tried to focus on cracking eggs into a big mixing bowl while Cam pulled big cast-iron pans out of a cupboard. Zoey could handle herself, and Blake's own mother was a gracious lady. And of course, Wren was adorable. Between them, they'd bring Carol Ann's mother around.

Maybe.

Cam leaned over and looked out the pass-through, too. He waved at his two sons and his wife, Jodi, who was carrying their baby on her hip. Cam was obviously a happy man, even though rumor had it he'd gone through a rough period with the boys' mother before he'd gotten together with Jodi.

"They're doing the gifts now, so we should hustle." Cam started breaking eggs, too.

"What gifts?" Blake asked as he got back to work.

"Some kind of a little plant in a decorated pot. Each kid made one for their mom." He frowned as he poured milk into the big bowl of raw eggs. "Sorry, man. Events like this have to be hard for you."

Blake felt like he was processing his own grief okay. Wren, though, cycled through feelings about losing her mother. Sometimes she barely seemed to remember Carol Ann; other times, the wound was raw. The family counselor he'd consulted after Carol Ann's death had warned hm that was likely to be the case.

Still, it was brutal on a father not to be able to protect his child from sadness and grief.

He watched the kids running to the table that held multiple flower pots with colorful ribbons tied around them and scraggly marigold plants inside the painted vessels.

Wren grabbed her plant, headed back to the table and gave the gift to Zoey.

"Uh-oh," Blake said, anticipating trouble.

Sure enough, both grandmas looked upset.

"I see your problem," Cam said beside him. "But it's probably better she gave it to Zoey rather than choosing one grandma over the other, right?"

"I guess." He watched as Zoey walked over to their mutual friend Kelly, who, in addition to wrangling her first graders and exclaiming over the plant her daughter, Zinnia, had given her, also seemed to be in charge of the overall plant giveaway. The two women spoke quietly. Then Zoey went and got Wren and brought her to the plant table, where Kelly handed her two additional plants in plain pots.

Wren skipped back to the table and presented them to her grandmothers.

Blake sighed. He had to hand it to Zoey for trying, but the damage was done.

Across the kitchen, someone was frying bacon, the smell wafting over and making Blake's stomach growl.

"So what's up with you and Zoey?" Cam shoved aside an empty egg carton. "You seem pretty close. Are you dating?"

"No!" Why was that idea coming up again?

"Alec said Zoey and Wren were at the diner the other night with you," he said. "And then Mrs. Henderson told me you drove her home."

"That's all true." Blake frowned. "She babysits for me, that's all." He found large containers of salt and pepper and brought them over.

Cam started shaking salt into the eggs. "No secrets in Holiday Point. Believe me, I know." Cam and Alec, along with their other two brothers, had grown up on the wild side, with a difficult family notorious for causing trouble in town.

And yet, both Cam and Alec had settled down and found happiness, which was more than Blake could say for himself.

Although that was wrong. Of course he'd found

happiness, with Carol Ann. It had just been yanked away from them too soon.

"Why don't you ask her out?" Cam suggested.

"Who, Zoey? No way!" Blake's face heated.

"What's the barrier? You guys are good friends, you're both single, she's very pretty and sweet."

Blake shook his head. "I'm not ready."

Cam shrugged and nodded. "Makes sense."

Blake's eyes kept being drawn back to Zoey, though, as the cooking continued and the breakfast was served.

Cam was right. She was pretty, and sweet, too. He wanted to protect her, to cushion some of the difficulties in her life. But that was just friendship, wasn't it?

Besides, Zoey was dating other people.

Which was great. Happy news, really. Good for her.

There was no reason on earth to feel upset about the fact that Zoey was going out with another man tomorrow night.

As soon as a few people started cleaning up from the Muffins with Mom event, Zoey jumped up to help.

What an uncomfortable morning. She hadn't considered, when she'd agreed to go, that she would have to sit with Wren's grandmothers.

Zoey had known Blake's mother ever since moving in with a foster family the next street over. Aside from being a little overprotective of her only son, she was a nice woman. She hadn't been thrilled when Wren had presented Zoey with the Mother's Day gift. But she'd managed to be pleasant, chatting with Zoey about Wren and the spring weather and upcoming specials at the diner.

Carol Ann's mom was another story. She'd acted surprised to see Zoey and shocked that Zoey would sit at the same table with them. "This area is for children and their families," she'd said coldly.

Zoey had had to explain that Wren had invited her, and the older woman's lips had pursed. Obviously, she thought that Zoey should have declined the invitation.

Wren came over to Zoey. "Can I help clean up?"

"Of course, honey. You're sweet to offer." Together, they pulled a rolling trash can over to the end of the long table where they'd been sitting and started tossing crumpled napkins and greasy paper plates into it. "Thank you, sweetie," she said, giving Wren a hug that felt almost defiant, given Mrs. Masterson's disapproval. "Why don't you go play with your friends for a little bit?"

Wren hugged her back and then rushed off toward a couple of little boys who were showing off martial arts moves to one another.

Zoey found a stack of paper towels and started wiping up spilled orange juice. Mrs. Masterson's attitude had thrust her right back into the past, when she'd been a new kid in town struggling with schoolwork that seemed impossible to understand. Carol Ann had started tutoring Zoey at her house, in her kitchen, since Zoey's foster home was noisy with lots of kids. Every time Carol Ann's mother had come into the kitchen and seen them, she'd turned up her nose. The moment Zoey collected her books to go home, Carol

Ann's mom would hurry and wipe off the table. She seemed to think Zoey might contaminate their house with her foster-kid dirt.

It had hurt Zoey enough that she'd talked Carol Ann into moving their sessions to the library after school.

Fast-forward to now, and Mrs. Masterson had lost her beloved daughter. Zoey felt for her and understood her desire to cling on to Wren as the only thing she had left of Carol Ann.

But did that mean Mrs. Masterson could make pointed remarks about Zoey's perfectly proper sweater and jeans, the same kind of attire that most of the young mothers were wearing? That the older woman could dig into how often Zoey was babysitting Wren and warn her against "getting any ideas" about dating Blake?

Ugh. Zoey was much happier wiping down tables than making nice with a not-nice woman.

"You shouldn't be doing that," one of the dads said. "Moms are supposed to take it easy today."

"Oh, she's not a mom," Mrs. Masterson said. "Don't you remember? She's that sweet little foster child my Carol Ann tutored."

The words hit Zoey right between the shoulder blades, sharp as a knife.

"Uh, well, you still don't have to clean up." The man gave Zoey an embarrassed smile and turned away.

"Be nice, Karen. She's a grown-up woman and a lovely one." Blake's mother patted Zoey's shoulder.

Zoey flashed her a smile and went looking for a broom, scolding herself for feeling hurt.

She *was* a former foster child. She wasn't all that bright; she'd needed help to make it through high school. She *wasn't* a mom.

She definitely wasn't the person Blake should have as a girlfriend, let alone a wife, and she wasn't the person Wren should have as a mom.

Mean Mrs. Masterson was right: she'd better not harbor any ideas to the contrary.

She started sweeping the floor, well coated with crumbs and fallen napkins.

Around her, kids ran and shouted, full of sugary muffins and reveling in the no-man's-land between the teachers' authority and their mothers'. Across the room, a janitor sprinkled sawdust over an area where a kid had gotten sick.

Zoey swept faster. She'd get this side of the floor done, and then she'd leave. Go get ready for work, where at least she felt respected and competent.

Blake came over and put a hand on the broom, stopping her. "You don't have to do that," he said. "Let me."

"You go talk to Wren and her grandmas," she said, holding on to the broom. "I'll do this. I don't mind."

She tried to start sweeping again, but he still held the broom. "Thank you for coming today. I really appreciate it."

She clenched her jaw. "Of course. Anything for Wren."

"I know it wasn't easy, hanging out with Wren's grandmothers," he continued.

Zoey glanced toward the table where the grand-mothers still sat.

Both of them were watching the exchange.

Mrs. Masterson's question about whether she wanted to date Blake pushed back into her mind. "I think you should go talk to them," she said. "Now." This time, she jerked the broom from his hands.

He tilted his head to one side. "Was it that bad?"

"Kinda." She backed away.

He let her go, but he was looking at her with con-cern. When she met his gaze, he didn't look away.

Zoey's heart fluttered and then settled into a rhyth-mic thudding. What was going on? This was *Blake.* Her good friend. Blake, who'd shown kindness to a disadvantaged, bullied child, but who was way, way out of her league.

"I do *so* have a mom!"

Wren's angry shout made both Zoey and Blake spin around. Two little girls stood on one side of a table and Wren on the other, facing them down.

Zoey and Blake rushed over, the grandmothers right behind them.

"I have *three* moms!" Wren said. She pointed at Zoey, then at each of her grandmothers. "One, two, three!"

Blake knelt beside Wren and put an arm around her. "Settle down, honey. You're okay."

"Three moms!" she insisted.

"That's not right, honey," Carol Ann's mom said. "We're your grandmothers. And she…" She nodded toward Zoey. "She's the babysitter. Your mommy's in heaven." Her voice went high and tight on the last words, and she turned away. Blake's mother patted her on the back, murmuring soothing words.

One of the little girls who'd been arguing with Wren had been whisked away by her apologetic father, but the other one remained. "See?" she said quietly. "You don't have a mommy."

Wren pulled away from Blake and rushed over to Zoey. She threw her arms around Zoey's legs. "I *will* have a mommy. I will! And it's gonna be *her*!"

Chapter Three

Blake hugged his daughter and wiped her tears with a napkin he'd grabbed from a nearby table. "It's okay to be sad about Mommy," he said. "It's okay to wish she could be here. I wish she could, too."

Around them, the cafeteria sounds were fading. Thankfully, the second little girl who'd rubbed in Wren's motherless status had gone away with her class.

Wren buried her face in Blake's chest. "I don't have a mommy. It's not fair!"

His heart ached. "It's hard to understand why she had to die," he said. "I know it hurts."

She nodded, her face still against his chest.

He stroked her hair, his throat tight.

He looked up to see that both of Wren's grandmothers, and Zoey, stood in a semicircle around them. Zoey pulled out a packet of tissues. She handed one to Blake, then passed them over to the other women, both of whom looked a little teary.

For a minute, he thought Carol Ann's mother would turn down the offer, but a tear ran down her face and she took a tissue and dabbed at her eyes.

Wren pulled back from his chest, and he wiped her tears and brushed a hand over her hair. Across the room, he could see her teacher lining up her classmates.

"Hug your grandmas and Zoey," he said. "Then it's time to go back to class. Your teacher told me you get to go outside to play later." He'd talked to her teacher about the fact that Wren had lost her mother, of course, when Wren had started school. He'd reminded her about it today, after the disaster of the plant gifts, and she'd reassured him that there were no more Mother's Day activities planned.

Wren hugged each grandma and Zoey and then ran over to her classmates. Blake sent up a quick prayer of thanks for the way kids could shift gears so readily.

That wasn't so much the case for adults. He felt drained emotionally, and as he got to his feet, he could see that the grandmas and Zoey felt the same.

"I'm going to say hi to Mary," his mother said and walked toward one of the cafeteria ladies who went to their church.

"Well," Zoey said, "nice to see you all. I'm headed to work." She didn't look at any of them, including Blake; she just turned and made for the door.

"Zoey—" He started after her. It wasn't right that her kind deed had resulted in such awkwardness.

Carol Ann's mother gripped his arm, stopping him. "Is there something going on between you and that woman?"

Blake looked after Zoey. She'd stopped to talk with Jodi, Cam's wife. If he didn't know her so well, he would have thought her smile was genuine. But he could read the strain on her face and the slight slump of her shoulders. She was upset.

"Well, is there?" Karen asked.

He looked at the woman and memories flooded him. Her happy expression at his and Carol Ann's wedding, which he'd eventually figured out was more her dream than Carol Ann's. Her criticisms of him as a husband, which weren't wrong; he hadn't been the best at it.

Her joy when Wren was born. Her breakdown at Carol Ann's funeral.

That memory brought back his own anguish at the funeral, anguish that was a mixture of grief and guilt. He and Carol Ann had been fighting more and more and had been planning to start counseling. And then she'd had her aneurysm and died.

The doctors had told him that the tragedy of her death was random and not caused by stress.

In his heart, though, he blamed himself. He'd done enough reading to know that Carol Ann's unhappiness with the marriage, which hadn't turned out as she wanted, could have caused high blood pressure and led, indirectly, to the aneurysm developing and rupturing.

He'd been a bad husband, which equated to being a bad man. And look at him now; he was letting Zoey go off alone and in pain after she'd done him and Wren a kind favor.

The cafeteria was nearly empty now, as teachers herded the remaining kids into lines and led them away. The smell of something like hot dogs wafted through the air. The cooks, the real ones, were preparing lunch for the kids.

"That Zoey is *not* what I want for my granddaughter," Karen said. "She's a waitress in a diner. You need to find a different babysitter and stop giving that poor woman hope that you'll get together with her."

Blake felt his eyebrows draw together. "That's not what's going on."

"Yes, it is. She's angling for your status and money."

Blake almost laughed, except that the attitude behind Karen's words wasn't funny.

There was no reasoning with her. No use in reminding her how disappointed she'd been to discover that a math professor at a small college didn't have a whole lot of either status *or* money. Still, he felt he had to defend his best friend. "Zoey has been wonderful with Wren. I'm fortunate, Wren's fortunate, to have her."

Karen drew in a breath, obviously ready to continue putting Zoey down. But Blake was watching Zoey.

Would the negative comments from Carol Ann's mother be enough to push her away?

The thought made him panicky. He and Wren couldn't lose Zoey. "Excuse me," he said to Karen and hurried across the cafeteria. Zoey had turned away from Jodi and was walking toward the door.

"Zoey," he called. "Wait."

She turned, her face closed. "I'm working the lunch shift at the diner today. I need to go."

"I'm sorry for all that," he said, gesturing back toward where Wren's little drama had taken place.

She sighed. "It's okay, Blake, but maybe we should figure out how to stop Wren from thinking that I'll be her mommy. Obviously, that's never going to happen."

Obviously, that's never going to happen. The words felt like a door slamming shut.

Why, though? He'd never attempted to date Zoey,

never had a thought that she'd become his wife and Zoey's mom.

Well, maybe a thought or two. But nothing serious. He didn't intend to marry again. Not Zoey, not anybody.

But they'd be friends forever, right?

Except that Zoey had a date coming up, a date with another man. If Zoey started seeing someone seriously, he and Wren would become secondary in her life, maybe even pushed out entirely. Desperation rose in him. "We promised Wren we'd take her to Danny Shelton's graduation party on Saturday." Danny was an adult student Blake had been mentoring at the college. He lived in a small town nearby, and Wren adored his twin boys. Zoey was a friend of the family, too, and had been invited. "You're still coming, aren't you? Wren will be upset if you don't."

Way to be manipulative. Some friend you are.

Zoey sighed. "Okay, Blake, fine. I'll see you Saturday." She turned and walked away, double time.

Blake's stomach twisted. What if he was losing Zoey? The thought made him feel terrible, desolate.

Maybe more than he should feel, if Zoey was really just a friend.

On Thursday night, Zoey studied the cans of soup in her cupboard. Then she closed it without taking one out to cook for dinner. She sat down on the couch, turned on the television and then turned it off.

After the disastrous Mother's Day breakfast, she'd gone to work, forced herself to smile and be attentive to her customers, made good tips. Then she'd done errands. Staying busy always helped her feel better.

Now, though, thoughts of Blake rushed back.

Normally, when she thought about Blake, she'd give him a call or stroll over to see him. But after the comments she'd heard today, from Carol Ann's mother and from Wren, her relationship with Blake didn't feel relaxed and easy like usual.

She wasn't going to go visit him. No way. That would just prove she was as needy as Carol Ann's mother had implied.

But not being able to see Blake left a bigger hole in her evening than it should have. Left her feeling a little blue, actually.

Which was ridiculous. She had plenty to do, plenty of friends. Plus, after a busy day, she'd earned the right to relax.

She'd just picked up one of her new library books when there was a knock on her door. Her heart leaped. Maybe Blake had come to her.

She opened the door to find her friends Kelly and Jodi. Kelly balanced a couple of boxes, one of them pizza-sized, and Jodi held a quart of ice cream. Disappointment and relief washed over Zoey, twin streams of conflicting emotion.

She held the door for them. "Hi, come in! I'm glad to see you, but…did I forget something? Did we have plans?"

"No," Kelly said, "but after the morning you had, we figured you need your friends."

"So we're inviting ourselves over for dinner," Jodi said.

Zoey's heart warmed. She did need friends, and not the complicated, Blake type of friends. She led the way into the kitchen.

Kelly set down the pizza, and Jodi stuck the ice cream in the freezer compartment of Zoey's fridge.

"I brought cookies, too," Kelly said. She held up a nicely wrapped box. Kelly had a side hustle baking and was seriously good at it.

Zoey pulled out plates and a pitcher of iced tea. "You guys are really sweet. But you didn't need to do this."

Kelly ignored the statement. "I was so mad I could spit," she said, "when I heard that awful woman saying 'she's the little foster child.'"

"And 'just the babysitter,'" Jodi contributed. She opened the pizza box, grabbed a spatula and started serving up hot slices. The smell of spicy tomato sauce and crisp, wood-fired crust spread through the room.

After the three of them had sat down and said a quick prayer, Zoey took a bite of pizza and closed her eyes. "Delicious. This is just what I was hungry for. Thank you!" She paused, then added, "And you know, technically, it's true that I'm a former foster child and that I'm Wren's babysitter. Mrs. Masterson wasn't wrong."

"But you're so much more than that," Kelly said.

Jodi wiped her mouth and nodded. "It sounded very dismissive."

"That's a good word for it," Zoey said, glad to have a way to describe what had annoyed her about Mrs. Masterson's comments. "I just wanted to help Wren get through Mother's Day. It's a hard holiday when you don't have a mom."

Kelly's face softened, and she squeezed Zoey's hand. "I wish you didn't know that from experience. She lost her mom, for all intents and purposes, really young," she added to Jodi, who hadn't known Zoey well growing up.

"I'm sorry to hear that. It must have been hard. Is that why you went into foster care?"

Zoey nodded. "So you can see why I want to help Wren. Although I'm not sure it turned out to be much help."

"It's honorable and sweet that you want to help that little girl," Kelly said. "But don't forget about your own needs. What do *you* want?"

Zoey paused, her slice of pizza halfway to her mouth. "What do you mean, what do I want?"

"In the personal area," Kelly clarified. "I mean, I thought I wanted to learn how to be a happy single. But underneath, I really wanted love and a family."

"That's what I want, too," Zoey blurted out, then felt her cheeks go hot. "I don't usually admit it, because I doubt I'm going to get it."

"Why?" Jodi asked.

Zoey shrugged. "I just… Men don't like me that way."

Jodi frowned. "Is that your foster care background talking?"

"Is it Blake and Wren you want as your family?" Kelly pressed.

"Well, I mean…" Zoey broke off. Kelly's question

was too confusing, so she addressed Jodi's. "I suppose it has to do with the way I kind of got lost in my foster family."

"Blake and Wren?" Kelly repeated. "Is there any chance *they* could become your family? You guys are so close."

She shook her head quickly. "I don't want to think about that because it's not going to happen. Blake would never fall for me. He's the type to marry another professor, and that would be good for Wren."

"Then you need to move on," Jodi said briskly.

At the same time, Kelly said, "I wouldn't be so quick to dismiss Blake. He's still healing from his loss, but I've seen the way he looks at you. I think he cares for you."

Zoey's heart beat a little faster. *How does he look at me?*

But contemplating that would just lead to heartache. "We're friends," Zoey said firmly. "We do care about each other. But that's as far as it's going to go. And all the speculation is hurting Wren."

"I see what you mean," Kelly said reluctantly.

"Anyway," Zoey said, wanting to get them off the topic of Blake, "I have a date tomorrow night."

They both squealed. "With who?" Kelly asked.

"He's a cook at the restaurant." She told them about Larry.

"Well, I for one am glad," Jodi said. "You deserve happiness."

"And you don't deserve to be put down by Blake's old in-laws," Kelly added.

They cleaned up the meal. Kelly and Jodi chatted about their kids, and before she knew it, Zoey was participating in the mom-style conversation with stories about Wren.

Maybe that was why the topic of Zoey's desire for a family came back up.

"You have to decide what you want and go after it," Kelly said.

"And whatever you do, we're here for you," Jodi added.

Their sympathy wasn't empty. Kelly had had two broken engagements, and Jodi's first marriage had been awful. They'd earned their happy endings.

"You guys are the greatest," she said. "Thanks so much for coming over. I feel a lot better."

They all hugged. "We feel for you," Kelly said. "And we're praying for you."

"Have fun on your date!" Jodi waggled her eyebrows up and down.

"But don't give up on Blake," Kelly added.

"Thank you guys, so much." As she ushered them out, Zoey realized she felt much better. Cared for and loved.

But still confused. Full of mixed feelings, both about her date tomorrow night, and about her plan to see Blake and Wren at Saturday's graduation party.

Chapter Four

Blake arrived home from work early on Friday afternoon, well before Wren was expected home from school. He fixed himself a sandwich and ate it standing up at the counter, skimming through the mail that had accumulated over a busy week.

He was *not* going to think about Zoey.

It was no use ruminating about yesterday's disastrous Mother's Day event. He needed to focus on getting Wren through her new awareness of what was missing in her life. Getting her through it *without* encouraging her to focus on Zoey as a potential new mom.

He glanced out the window, and his resolution not to think about Zoey blew away on the spring breeze.

She was outside in the backyard of her rental, planting flowers. Her hair was pulled back, and she wore a T-shirt and faded jeans. Without making the least effort to dress up, she looked gorgeous.

He swallowed hard as Zoey's words came back to him: they needed to stop Wren from thinking that Zoey could be her mom. *That's never going to happen.*

She was right, of course. He'd decided immediately after Carol Ann's death that he wouldn't marry again. Truthfully, it hadn't been a hard resolution to make.

Marriage had been difficult for him, and he'd had a constant feeling of failure.

His permanent single status wasn't news to him, so why did it make his heart twist and ache now?

He watched as Zoey shoveled mulch into a wheelbarrow, then pushed the heavy load toward the flower bed. Her slender, muscular arms strained with the task.

Abandoning the rest of his sandwich, he headed down the stairs. He marched across the yard, took the wheelbarrow from her and pushed it to the garden. "How come you're putting in the flowers this year? Your landlord should do that."

"He's giving me a break on the rent this month. Thanks for the help, though." She studied the spindly seedlings she'd planted in clusters. "Besides, I love yard work and flowers."

He knew that; she'd helped him with weeding for the past couple of summers. He started shoveling mulch into the little garden. "I'll do the grunt work. You spread it where you want it."

"You don't have to do that." But she knelt and used a small digger to tuck the mulch in between the seedlings.

He sought for a reason to keep working beside her and quickly found one. "We need to troubleshoot about Wren's desire for you to be her mom."

She glanced up at him. Her cheeks were pink, whether from the idea or from exertion he couldn't tell. A stray strand of wavy brown hair blew across her face, and she used the back of a knuckle to push it behind her ear. "Maybe it'll fade naturally after this weekend. Mother's Day is hard for kids who don't have a mom."

The words triggered a memory. When Zoey had first moved to town, it had been this time of year. On Mother's Day, after church and a quiet brunch with his parents, he'd been riding his bike around the neighborhood when he'd heard a sound coming from the bushes. Thinking it was a kitten, he'd veered toward it and then realized it was the new girl. She'd been hunched over, arms wrapped around her knees, crying.

As an awkward adolescent, he hadn't been especially good at emotions, so he'd ridden away before Zoey had seen him. Later, he'd told his mother that the new girl was upset. She'd shaken her head. "She's moved around quite a bit, and now her parents lost custody of her, from what Mrs. Cannon said. Poor child. Only time will heal that wound."

He supposed his mother had been right. Zoey seemed healthy and happy now. "Do you think Wren will get over losing her mom, with time?" he asked her.

Zoey stood, her expression thoughtful. "Maybe," she said. "You should probably talk to her, though. Explain that she may get a new mommy one day, but it won't be me."

The words hurt him, and he emptied the wheelbarrow of mulch with record speed. Working with his muscles didn't remove the ache in his heart, but at least it gave him something else to think about.

"Or maybe," she said lightly, "Wren needs to see

us with other people. Isn't there a professor at the college you'd like to date?"

No one as pretty and good as you. "No," he barked out.

She ignored his answer. "Maybe you'll meet someone at the graduation party tomorrow. There should be some women from the college there, right? I'll be your wingman if you need."

"Not really interested."

"If you're looking for a way to help Wren... But it's your call. Thanks for helping with the mulch." She brushed her hands on the sides of her jeans. "I need to go in and get ready for *my* date tonight."

Another knife to the gut. He leaned on the shovel and watched her walk away.

He didn't understand his feelings for Zoey. She was his longtime friend, a more and more important friend. But that was all she was, and all she could be.

He knew it in his head, but no matter how often he reminded himself, his heart couldn't seem to retain the information.

At ten thirty Friday night, Zoey thanked Larry for taking her out, evaded his attempt at an embrace and went inside her house. She leaned against the door and listened for the sound of his truck starting up and driving away. Then she walked straight through the house and out the back door. She strolled down toward the river.

Moonlight made the water shine like hammered silver, and the smell of newly awakening earth soothed her senses. The cry of a lone bird sounded over the lapping water.

She wanted love and a family. To move toward that goal, she needed to date.

But tonight had been a disappointment. She'd struggled to connect with Larry amidst the multiple TV screens and excited fans in the sports bar where he'd taken her. When they *had* talked, she'd learned that in addition to team sports, he liked hunting and fishing. Besides the restaurant, they had little in common.

It had been nothing like talking to Blake. With him, conversation flowed easily from mundane topics to spiritual ones.

She sank onto a big rock that overlooked the water. She was just a waitress, as Carol Ann's mother had said. She was intellectually average. She had nothing to offer a man like Blake.

But she couldn't get involved with a guy like Larry, whose interests were so different from hers. *What do I do, Lord?*

Moments later, as some of God's peace settled around her, she heard a soft voice. "Hey, could you use a s'more?"

Blake. Just the sound of his voice made her calmer, happier. She couldn't keep the smile from her face as she stood and turned. "What are you doing out here so late?"

"Just restless. Wren's asleep. She had a friend over, and we built a fire and made s'mores. There's plenty of marshmallows and everything else left, and I still have hot coals. Want a late-night snack?"

The thought of spending a little bit of time with Blake was more soothing than the night sounds around her. But was it wise, given the way she'd been feeling?

"Come on," he said. "You can tell me about your date."

"Well…" She did want to. "Okay, I'll come over for a few minutes. And one s'more."

He led the way to the firepit behind his house and gestured toward the lawn chairs beside it. "So how was it?" he asked as he opened a paper grocery bag and pulled out a bag of marshmallows.

"Not great. He was disappointed that I don't drink. And I was disappointed that he took me to a loud, rowdy sports bar. But it was just as well, because it turns out we have nothing in common except for work."

"Did he drink too much?" Blake asked sharply.

She shook her head. "Not at all. He had one beer. He's a good guy, just not for me."

Blake poked at the coals and then threaded a couple of marshmallows onto a stick. He handed it to her, then made a duplicate for himself and knelt next to the fire.

She pulled her chair forward, and they held their marshmallows over the hot orange coals. A small flame leaped up, then died down again. A gusty breeze brought cool air, and Zoey leaned closer to the warmth of the fire.

"It's hard to find someone compatible," Blake said.

She looked sideways at him. "For me it is. You were blessed."

"What do you mean?"

"Just that Carol Ann was so smart. You had a lot in common, way beyond the fact that you grew up in the same town. You must have had things to talk about all the time."

He looked into the fire and turned his marshmallows. "We had more angry silences than great conversations toward the end." He paused, then added, "I'm not putting her down. It was entirely my fault."

"Hmm." Zoey thought back. She hadn't spent much time with Blake and Carol Ann socially, but she'd been in and out of their home as a babysitter. Now that she thought about it, she hadn't heard them talking to each other all that much. "You had a young child. It was probably hard to get a lot of couple time to talk."

But then again, Zoey had always found Blake easy to talk with. Even when Wren was acting up, he joked around and made things fun. "It probably wasn't all your fault."

He sighed and shook his head. "No, it was. I was a bad husband."

"Really?" She studied him. "That's weird, because you're a pretty great guy."

Then her face went hot. Who was she to be saying such a thing? Would he take it as a friendly comment or misinterpret it as her wanting more from their relationship?

And would that even *be* a misinterpretation?

"I'm really not a great guy." He broke graham crackers, topped them with chocolate and then used another graham cracker to slide toasted marshmallows in between. He gestured for her to hand him her stick and did the same for her, making a gooey s'more and handing it to her.

They crunched in silence, but it was comfortable. That was what was so good about being longtime friends. You could talk or not.

She stole a glance at his profile. Strong jaw, straight nose, thick eyebrows and hair. He was too bulky and rough-hewn to be what her friends considered hot, but he was attractive.

He caught her staring. "You got marshmallow in your hair," he said, touching a strand of it.

She lifted her hand to feel the slight stickiness. Their gaze hadn't broken. She sucked in a breath.

He leaned closer.

Her heart hammered. In the firelight, his eyes glowed, then softened. He caught her hand in his.

This is *Blake*. Your best friend.

She jumped to her feet. "Well, better go in. Thanks for the s'more," she said. She walked rapidly into her house, her pulse still racing.

How come it had been so very easy to rebuff Larry's effort at a hug...and so hard not to lean right in and kiss Blake?

Chapter Five

What was happening to his friendship with Zoey?

It was Saturday. They'd just arrived at his student's graduation party, Blake driving, Zoey beside him, Wren in the back seat. His focus should have been on his student and his happiness about the promising young man's graduation. Instead, he kept thinking about last night.

He had almost kissed her!

He'd touched her hair, and she'd looked at him with wide eyes, and he'd lost his mind. Maybe it was the firelight, or the starry sky above, but he'd felt an overwhelming urge to pull her into his arms.

He was pretty sure she'd read that intention, and she'd literally run away.

Now it was awkward between them. Their conversation, which usually flowed, was halting and mundane. Several times, they both started talking at the same time, and then fell quiet.

He was grateful for Wren's chatter.

Grateful when they finally arrived at the party.

Danny lived with his parents and his daughters in a big, old house. The yard was brightly decorated with banners and balloons and filled with loud, pulsing music. Wren saw the twins and ran to them. Blake started to follow her.

"Wait," Zoey said.

He turned back instantly, an absurd hope in his chest, hope for something he couldn't even articulate.

"You know," she said, "you really should try to date."

"What?" Did she mean he should date *her*?

"You should try to date," she repeated patiently. "So Wren sees you with someone else besides me."

"But I don't want to—"

"It's for Wren," she said firmly. "You need to find a like-minded woman, and where better than a party with people from the college?"

He tried to cover his deflated feeling with a smile that felt forced. "I'm not sure my trolling for dates at a party is going to make a difference to her," he said. "She wants *you*."

And so do I.

The realization hit him hard. It wasn't just that he liked her as a friend. It wasn't just that he'd gotten attracted on a moonlit night. He wanted Zoey.

But because he cared for her, he wasn't going to pursue a relationship with her. He was too bad of a partner, of a husband, for that.

Carol Ann's scathing comments rang in his head. *Too selfish. Too clingy. Too pushy.*

What he thought of as a marriage, his own parents' close and affectionate connection, had been way too much for Carol Ann. Or maybe he'd had unrealistic expectations, as she'd often said.

Zoey was looking at him, one hand on her hip. "I tried dating someone else already. It's your turn." She turned and headed toward Wren and the other kids.

All around were happy people enjoying food and drinks, loud music and shouted conversation. The sun beat down warm on the top of his head. Wren played happily with her friends.

Maybe Zoey was right. Maybe Wren needed to see him with another woman, or several, so that she'd get off her Zoey kick.

Maybe that would get him off *his* Zoey kick, too. Last night had been too, too risky. He couldn't repeat that mistake again.

He supposed he should try to take out some nice woman who wouldn't get overly attached.

He wandered through the party, greeting people, getting into longer conversations with a couple of his favorite colleagues. He found Danny and clapped him on the back, shook his hand. He put his graduation card into the little bin on a side table, knowing that any amount of money would be a help to the young father as he started on his professional journey.

"Hey, Blake, wait up!"

Zoey's voice sounded like sunshine, and he turned. She was walking toward him with a woman he half recognized.

"Blake," Zoey said, "this is Sharlene. She's the mom of a four-year-old who's a real cutie, and she teaches in the psychology department. Have you two met?"

He shook the woman's hand. "We haven't met one-on-one, I don't think," he said. "I saw you introduced at the faculty meeting at the beginning of the year, but our paths haven't crossed since."

"And I've met so many people I get confused,"

Sharlene said, smiling. "I think we all attend the same church, though I usually go to the early service. That way, I can get to my paper-grading earlier."

He nodded in sympathy. "The first year is the hardest," he said. "I hope they don't have you serving on too many committees already?"

"Seems like I'm in on every diversity-related meeting, but it's fine. Goes with the job."

They chatted on about the joys and perils of being a new professor on the tenure track.

Zoey watched them chat for a few minutes, her smile fixed. Then she broke in. "Looks like the kids are getting restless," she said. "I'll take them over to the bouncy house. You two talk."

"It's okay, I can come—" Sharlene started to say.

"You don't have to—" Blake said at the same time.

"Not a problem," Zoey interrupted both of them. She turned and walked toward a group of kids that included Danny's twins, Wren and another little girl.

"Is that your daughter?" he asked, and Sharlene nodded.

He tore his eyes away from Zoey and tried to be attentive to Sharlene. They chatted pleasantly about being single parents and about the schools in the area.

Blake kept looking over toward the bouncy house, and finally, Sharlene tapped his arm. "Let's walk over there," she said. As they headed in that direction, she nudged him. "How long have you been in love with her?"

"What?" He blinked.

"How long," she said patiently, "have you been in love with Zoey?"

He stopped walking. "I'm not in love with her."

"You can't stop looking at her."

"No, you don't understand," he said. "She's my good friend. That's all."

"You should ask her out," Sharlene said. "Sorry to be intrusive, but it goes with being a psychologist. You're saying one thing, but your body language says something else entirely. Ask her out."

Blake clenched his jaw. He was trying *not* to do that. This type of pressure wasn't helping.

Why did everyone seem to want to tell him what to do about his love life?

"Pray about it first," Sharlene amended. "And then trust your heart."

"Thanks for the suggestion," he said, keeping his voice even.

His heart seemed to be the one thing that couldn't be trusted.

Somehow, the tables had turned on Zoey.

Sharlene had insisted on taking Wren and her own daughter to get hot dogs. By herself. Zoey and Blake were left alone amongst the pulsing music, young people dancing and laughing and warm May sunshine.

By mutual unspoken agreement, they backed out of the crowd and found a table away from the speakers. Neither of them liked loud music.

"Did you ask her out?" she demanded of Blake.

He shook his head. "No."

Happiness filled Zoey despite her efforts to resist it. Sharlene was so pretty, so sweet and so obviously a super-brain like Blake. It had almost killed Zoey to introduce her and Blake, but she'd done it.

"Why not?" she asked.

He shrugged, his expression evasive. "I just didn't feel it. She's a nice person, though. We might become friends."

"That's one route to getting together."

The sentence seemed to hang in the air as their eyes met. Zoey knew exactly what he was thinking because she was thinking the same thing herself.

They were friends. At first, that was all they'd been. More and more, though, it was hard to ignore the chemistry developing between them.

Like now, as they gazed at each other.

Blake's eyes were brown, with a golden ring around the pupils. His lashes were thick and dark, like his hair and eyebrows. In all the years she'd known him, it was the first time she'd noticed these things about him.

Maybe because she never dared to look so closely.

Zoey sucked in a breath and wrapped her fingers around the edge of the stone bench, welcoming its hard coldness. She looked at the canopy of weeping cherry blossoms overhead. The sounds of birds, and adults talking, and kids shouting, faded away.

There was just now, this moment that she didn't want to end. Drinking in the intensity and wonder of Blake.

He seemed to move a few inches toward her, which was a terrible idea. They were on the edge of a crowd.

Weren't they supposed to be trying to convince Wren, and everyone, that they *weren't* a couple?

She saw a friend from church looking at them. Another.

They weren't doing a very good job.

Fortunately, people standing nearest to the porch started clinking on glasses to get everyone's attention. Zoey and Blake stood and walked closer as people spoke up about Danny's achievement. Danny thanked people, including Blake, and then his twins ran up and threw their arms around their father. He was still wearing his graduation cap, kneeling down to hug his girls, and people started lifting phones to snap the adorable image.

When Danny left the limelight, he came right over to Blake and hugged him. "I couldn't have done this without you. Thanks, man."

"I may have coached a little from the sidelines, but you won the game yourself," Blake said. "Call me next week. I might have a lead on a job opportunity for you."

Danny's face lit up. "Will do!"

As Danny moved on, other colleagues and students gravitated toward Blake. Zoey went to a nearby bench and watched as he talked with them. He was animated, popular, in his element. She remembered him from his teenage years and could barely fathom how far he'd come. She was proud of him and she adored watching him, but she felt almost ashamed of that.

It was the twenty-first century. The time of women

adoring their much-more-successful men, watching them shine from the sidelines, was long gone.

Women were, or should be, equally on center stage.

Zoey knew she was good at what she did, but no one would ever sing her praises for it. No one would look at her with the kind of admiration Blake commanded effortlessly.

Sharlene was part of the crowd talking and laughing, and Zoey noticed that Blake purposely directed comments her way, making sure his newer colleague was included.

Sharlene was much better suited to Blake than Zoey was.

Sharlene's little girl, Alicia, came rushing over to her mom, holding Wren's hand. Zoey started to stand so she could keep the little ones from distracting their parents, but Sharlene backed up a few steps, knelt down and listened.

Then she smiled broadly and nodded. She took Wren by the shoulder and pointed toward Zoey.

Wren ran over. "Miss Zoey! You're going to sit with us at church!"

"With who, honey?"

"With me and Alicia and Alicia's mom," she said. "And Daddy."

"Maybe." Zoey was reserving judgment on that one.

"No, you have to," Wren insisted. "It's a Mother's Day thing, and you hafta be my mother!"

Here we go again. Two possible scenarios, neither very appealing, fast-forwarded on her mind's screen.

Maybe she'd sit behind Blake and Sharlene, taking care of their children while they conducted their romance.

Or maybe Wren would announce to the congregation that Zoey was her mommy.

It could truly go either way. At least she wouldn't feel her usual Mother's Day gloom if she had all that going on. *Thanks a lot, God*, she said internally, shooting a glare at the sky.

Chapter Six

That evening after the graduation party, Blake tried to focus on putting Wren to bed. But his mind was on Zoey.

He'd asked her to stick around for a few minutes so they could talk. Now, he had to go through with it.

Wren, her face washed, teeth brushed and prayers recited, was telling him a long, involved story about an earthworm the kids had found at the party. He leaned back against the headboard, his arm around her as she cuddled next to him, and tried to listen.

His mind wandered back to the party.

Zoey had wanted him to ask Sharlene out, but he hadn't been able to do it. Just didn't have the interest, and it wouldn't be fair to Sharlene.

Why didn't he have the interest, though? Sharlene was pretty, seemed kind, had a child near Wren's age and worked at the university. They should have been a match.

But they weren't. And moreover, Sharlene had accused him of being in love with Zoey.

That wasn't possible. He did find Zoey attractive—increasingly so—but she was his best friend. He couldn't stand to lose that friendship, which was exactly what would happen if they took things further and she realized what a sorry excuse for a boyfriend, let alone husband, he would be.

Life without Zoey was unimaginable. He didn't dare ruin their friendship by attempting to date her.

But for him to go on as he had been, in the two years since Carol Ann had died, was difficult, too.

He had to admit, he was lonely for the kind of companionship a wife would offer. More importantly, Wren wanted a mother.

Sticking to his plan of remaining single was getting more difficult, but he didn't know what else to do.

"Read this one, Daddy?" Wren had pulled a book from the shelf beside her bed, and she handed it to him. When he saw the title, he winced. *Are You My Mother?*

The child knew how to stick to a theme, that was for sure.

He could only hope Wren's obsession with finding a mother would fade once the holiday had passed. Then surely, her attention would flit to something else.

They just had to get through church tomorrow and the luncheon afterward.

He thought back to the past couple of Mother's Days. He'd gone numbly through the motions that first year; he could barely remember it. He'd been lost in a flurry of sadness and guilt and the effort to parent a grieving three-year-old alone.

Last year, he'd been grateful for the family and church events that gave him and Wren companionship and something to do. Wren had been happy to see her grandparents and cousins, and she'd lived in the moment like any respectable four-year-old, not thinking about what she'd lost in the past.

This year, her focus on the holiday seemed to mark a new phase in her development. He had to try his best to help her through it without rousing any hopes that Zoey could be her mother.

As he turned the last page, Wren's eyes fluttered shut.

He sat another couple of minutes, treasuring the sweet child beside him. Then he eased his way out of the bed, tucked Wren into the warm covers and started downstairs.

Halfway down, he stopped.

The floor was clear of toys, and the fleece blanket was neatly folded on the back of the couch. A mason jar full of lilacs sat on the end table, the sweet fragrance wafting toward him.

It was Zoey's doing.

He loved it. Loved a woman's touch in his home, although Carol Ann would have called him on the sexist notion. Men could clean and decorate. He ought to work harder at it than he did.

Especially considering there wasn't going to *be* a permanent woman's touch in their house.

There wasn't. There couldn't be. He had to remember that. But the thought filled him with bleakness.

Zoey came in from outside with a couple of small rugs in her hands. She put one down by the front door and straightened it.

She was probably horrified at what a mess his home had been, probably felt both obligated to help and upset about it.

He hurried the rest of the way down. "You didn't

have to do all this," he said. He took the second door-mat from her hands and carried it over to the side door. "I know these were pretty dirty, but it's not your job."

"They just needed a good shaking out," she said. "I like to stay busy."

"You don't resent housework?"

She laughed. "Honestly, when you come from a background like mine, you're mostly happy to have a home to fix up." She studied him, looking puzzled. "I get that some people don't like to clean, but why would you *resent* it?"

Blake could recite the reasons by heart. "Because it's unpaid labor that disproportionately falls on women," he said. "Because society still judges women by the state of their home, but not men." He smiled a little. "Those aren't my brilliant observations. I never noticed how my mom did everything around the house, I just enjoyed the benefits of it. And never learned to do any of it, because Mom thought that was women's work." He shrugged. "Carol Ann set me right about all of that."

"Well, Carol Ann had bigger fish to fry than cleaning a house," Zoey said, her voice mild. "So do you, for that matter."

"That's a matter of opinion. Sit down. I'll bring you a soda."

She didn't sit, though; she wandered into the kitchen after him. To his chagrin, he saw that the dishes had been put away, the floor swept.

Another vase of lilacs sat at the center of the kitchen table.

He brought over a couple of sodas and pulled out a kitchen chair for her. "Thank you for doing all this," he said. "Sit down. Relax. This is supposed to be your day off from being on your feet for eight-or ten-hour shifts at the diner."

She smiled then. "That's a good point. Okay."

He sat kitty-corner from her. "Besides, like I said, I need to talk with you. Can you spare me a few more minutes?"

"Sure, I guess." Her voice sounded suddenly wary.

Now he had no choice but to go through with it. He took a deep breath. "You tried to match me up with Sharlene," he said.

"Is it working?"

"No." He took a gulp of soda. *Say it.* "I don't know if you've noticed, but I feel some sparks between... us. You and me."

Her cheeks went pink as she nodded. "I have."

She'd noticed! And she didn't seem horrified at the idea. He had to tamp down the hope that rose in him.

Hope was the wrong thing to feel when they couldn't get together.

"Look, Zoey, your friendship is really important to me. That's why I need to explain the mixed messages I've been sending."

She studied him with a half smile, as if fascinated by what he was going to say next.

"There's a reason I can't, well, explore that. Though I'd like to." He looked down at the table and then focused his gaze on the lilacs. "Look, I was a really bad husband. I can't make a woman happy. So knowing that, I can't inflict myself on any woman. Especially one as important to me as you are." He leaned forward, sniffed the flowers and then looked at her. "But as you know, Wren wants a mom, so I'm in a pickle."

"You are." She tipped her head to one side and didn't say more.

He plowed on. "Thank you for stepping in, standing in, on all of these Mother's Day activities. But I won't expect you to do it in the future."

There. He'd gotten it all out.

Now there was no sound except the ticking of the old-fashioned clock on the wall.

Finally, she asked, "Why were you a bad husband?"

He'd thought a lot about that. "It's just a personal deficiency. I mean, I've always been more focused on numbers than people, and—"

"No," she interrupted. "I mean, what makes you think that you were a bad husband? Where did you get that idea?"

"Carol Ann told me. She pointed out that I put my own need for closeness and togetherness ahead of her need for space and independence."

She scratched at a rough spot on the table. "Carol Ann put her own needs first, too, didn't she?"

He thought about that. He'd been so busy scrambling to fix his own inadequacies that he hadn't considered his wife might share some of them. "Maybe she did," he said.

"It's a human tendency," Zoey said slowly. "I think most of us can be self-centered. But the key to a happy marriage is probably to always put the other person first. If both partners do that, things should work out okay." She shrugged. "Not that I'm some big expert. I've barely even dated."

"That's hard for me to understand." He was glad to take the spotlight off himself, but also puzzled. Why hadn't men flocked to Zoey?

She shrugged. "I think I put off a stay-away vibe, but I'm trying to change that."

"Because..." he prompted.

"Because I'd like to marry and have a family someday." She bit her lip. "But we're not talking about me, we're talking about you. I'm sorry to hear you and Carol Ann had problems. It sounds like normal growing pains, though."

He shrugged. "Maybe? I didn't do enough around the house," he added, intent on doing a full confession. "You can see it. My place gets pretty messy now."

One corner of her mouth curved upward. "That's an understatement. But didn't you and Carol Ann hire a cleaning service?"

"Yeah, for a little while." He'd hated that. "I didn't want to. We couldn't really afford it, and I thought it would be good to do it together rather than having someone else in the house doing it." He shrugged. "We tried cleaning together, but in the end, I'd get involved in work and forget to do my share."

She leaned forward. "Things like housework and chores, that's all on the surface," she said. "Are those the reasons you don't think you'd be a good husband?"

"I... Well." He got up, restless, and rinsed the soda cans, put them in the recycling bin. Loyalty to Carol

Ann kept him from explaining the worst of it: how Carol Ann had admitted she had been pushed into marriage by her mother, how she'd pulled away physically, how he'd pushed for them to be closer, but that had made her distance herself more in self-defense.

The thought of all the conflict made him sit down again, feeling sick. He sat down, head in his hands. "There was more, but I won't go into it. We'd just scheduled an appointment with a counselor when she had her aneurysm."

She reached out and squeezed his arm. "I'm so sorry."

"I blame myself."

"For the conflict? Or for her death?"

"Well, both."

She kept her hand on his arm, rubbed it gently. "You didn't cause it to happen. It was a random tragedy."

"Or maybe stress induced," he said. Needing to get away from the all-too-pleasant feeling of her hand on his arm, he scooted back his chair. It made a loud scraping noise as he stood.

"Did a doctor tell you that?" She looked up at him.

"No, but—"

"But you still blame yourself. You shouldn't." She stood and put her arms around him. "You're a good man, Blake. You deserve love in your life."

Her words, but even more than that, her gentle embrace, loosened something in him. She obviously believed it, believed in him. It was a balm.

He wrapped his arms around her, meaning to return the hug. But then he smelled the flowery scent of her. He felt her warmth. He slid his hands up her arms and felt their softness.

He heard her breath catch and pulled back to look into her face. His own heart was hammering. "I…" He felt he needed to apologize, except that she was the one who'd hugged him first.

He was pretty sure he was the one who wanted it more, though. He stepped back and took her hands. "Thanks for listening."

"Of course. I meant what I said." She reached up and touched his face. "You're a good man."

He caught her hand, turned it over and kissed it, like you'd give a child a kiss to hold.

This didn't feel anything like child's play, though. Her cheeks flushed. Her gaze tangled with his.

He knew, dimly, that he was making a mistake, but he didn't have the self-control to avoid it. Instead, he let himself kiss her knuckles. Her wrist.

She didn't pull away. Her lips parted a little. It almost seemed like she *wanted* his touch. Which would be…amazing. Way more than he could have asked for and more than he deserved.

He moved close enough to feel her breath on his cheek. He touched her face and took a half step closer. And stopped. "Is this okay?" he asked. The last thing he wanted to do was make Zoey uncomfortable.

She gave the slightest nod. And a tiny smile. Her eyes were warm, welcoming.

It was enough. He leaned in and kissed her.

Chapter Seven

Zoey melted into Blake's arms.

Who would have known that a man's caring touch could feel this amazing?

Blake kissed her with tenderness, but also decisively. Like he meant it; like he knew what he was doing. His arms felt strong around her.

She touched his hair, his neck, his muscular shoulders, realizing she'd been wanting to do so for months now. She breathed in the piney fragrance of the soap he used.

A cautionary alarm sounded somewhere in her head. *You're not suited to each other. You're not at his intellectual level. He can't really mean this.*

He lifted his head and looked at her, and for a moment they just stared into each other's eyes. Then he pulled her close again, this time holding her gently against his shoulder. "Oh, Zoey, Zoey. I've wanted to do that for a long time."

She closed her eyes and let herself dream that maybe, maybe this could work.

The next morning, she was still floating on cloud nine when she got a text from Blake.

Had to get to church early to help set up tables. See you there.

She dressed carefully in a dress the color of daffodils and curled her hair, letting it fall loose around her shoulders. She thought about wearing her strappy four-inch heels, but finally decided on simple wedges—a little nicer than what she wore for work or around the house, but not so dressy that she'd call attention to herself.

Still, Kelly, who was working as a greeter this morning, grasped her hands and looked her up and down. "You're glowing! What a pretty dress."

"Thanks." Zoey felt her cheeks go pink.

Blake emerged from the sanctuary, and even in the crowd milling around the church's entry, she saw him instantly and couldn't take her eyes off him.

He was so handsome, so smart, so kind.

And he'd chosen to kiss *her*.

Kelly turned to greet the next person, and Zoey moved toward Blake without even planning to, drawn by his magnetic force.

He spotted her and his eyes darkened, and she was glad she'd taken time with her appearance.

He touched her elbow. "Can you talk a minute?" His voice sounded serious.

"Um, sure." Flustered, wondering who was noticing them together, she followed him to an empty corner of the sanctuary.

"Look, Zoey." He met her eyes and then glanced away. "Last night was a mistake."

The sinking feeling inside her was like a hundred pounds of lead, settling on her heart. "O-kaay."

"I shouldn't have kissed you," he said in a rush.

"I never wanted to hurt you, but it's just not going to work between us. I can't remarry, and I shouldn't have touched you in that situation."

"I wasn't going to insist that you propose," she said, trying for humor.

He didn't smile, didn't even seem to hear her. "It just shows what a jerk I am."

To Zoey, it sounded like an excuse. Like the classic, "It's not you, it's me."

People were walking in now, sidling into pews, chatting in the aisles.

He means he can never marry me. *I don't suit him.*

Suddenly, Wren was there, wrapping her arms around Zoey's legs. "Come on, come on. We're sitting together."

She brushed a hand over Wren's hair and looked up at Blake. "Do you want me to sit somewhere else?"

"No, of course not." He sounded miserable.

Well, he should be miserable! He'd just dumped his best friend. And now he had to sit in church with her.

It served him right.

Only she was the one who was going to suffer, she realized as she followed Wren to a pew that already held Blake's parents, Sharlene and Sharlene's daughter. Wren climbed over her grandparents to get to Sharlene's daughter.

"I'll sit back here," she said, sliding into the pew behind the girls.

Sharlene smiled and reached back to grasp Zoey's hand. "I'm glad you came. You don't have to sit back there, though. Why don't you move up here? There's plenty of room."

Blake's parents turned to greet her, too. "Yes, come on up," Blake's father said in a hearty voice.

His mother didn't join the chorus. Nor did Blake. But Sharlene and Blake's father kept on insisting.

"Sure, okay," she said finally. She moved up to sit beside Wren just as several people moved out into the aisle to let a father and daughter scoot past them. In the reshuffling afterward, Zoey and Blake ended up next to each other, crowded in, thighs touching.

Great.

She tried to focus on the announcements and readings. Of course, there weren't enough hymnals. She debated with herself, then held hers open to share with Blake. But he didn't even look her way. Instead, he stood, singing the hymn by memory in his strong, deep voice.

When the offering plate was passed, he was careful not to touch her hand.

His standoffishness now made her realize how friendly and affectionate the two of them had started to be. It had evolved so naturally, she'd barely noticed. But it had made her happy. Now, the absence of warmth broke her heart.

Don't cry, don't cry.

It was what she'd always told herself when moved into a new foster home and new school. *Don't let them see that you're scared or upset. Pretend like everything's okay, like you're the happy, grateful foster kid.*

Sharlene's daughter snuggled up against Sharlene as the pastor talked about motherhood. Wren watched for a minute and then, experimentally, snuggled against

Zoey. Zoey put an arm around Wren and smiled down at her.

When she looked up, she saw Blake's mother shoot them a concerned look.

Blake himself focused entirely on what was going on at the front of the church, his jaw square, his expression rigid.

Hurt and anger warred inside her. She hadn't pushed herself on Blake, hadn't insinuated herself into his life with Wren. She'd just tried to help them as a neighbor and old friend.

Now look where it had gotten her. Not only did it seem like Mrs. Evans was blaming her, but Blake was definitely pulling away.

So was she losing her best friend?

This day, which had started out seeming so wonderful, was turning really, really bad.

Blake was mingling among the after-church crowd when he heard Wren's voice, floating in through the open doors.

Her *begging* voice. "Please, please, please," she was saying, tugging on both of Zoey's hands.

Blake hurried down the church steps and wove through the groups of churchgoers lingering to enjoy the brisk, sunny morning. He just needed to get through this day, get Wren through this day. Then he'd start to work with her on manners and behavior. It wasn't appropriate for her to whine for what she wanted, not at five years old.

"There's a lunch! For Mother's Day! You hafta

come!" Wren was speaking to Zoey, who'd knelt in front of her.

He reached the pair. "Wren. No whining." Though he felt like whining for Zoey to come to the after-church luncheon, himself.

Zoey looked up at him and stood. Gently, she tugged her hands away from Wren's. "I'm sorry, honey. I can't come this time."

After that once glance, she didn't look at him again, but he still felt awful. He'd hurt her. Badly. She'd opened herself to him, let him kiss her, and it had been such a beautiful kiss.

And then he'd coldly shut her off. He couldn't blame her for not wanting to be around him and Wren anymore.

She hugged Wren and then walked away, her yellow dress glowing in the sun. More than one man glanced her way and took a second look. Zoey the friendly waitress had morphed into Zoey the gorgeous woman.

He wanted to run after her, to beg forgiveness, to hold her in his arms.

"Blake!"

Dutifully, he turned away from Zoey and toward his parents, who were beckoning to him.

"Aren't you concerned about Wren's attachment to Zoey?" his mother asked.

I'm concerned about my *attachment to Zoey.* "I'm more worried about the way she's expressing it," he said. "I need to work with her on taking no for an answer."

"You'd better stop inviting Zoey to things," Blake's father said.

"People are starting to talk," his mother added.

"I hate to say it, but maybe Karen's right. Zoey's a sweet young woman, but unless you're planning to date her, she shouldn't be getting that close to Wren." She looked past him. "Is that the Mastersons' car? He's driving too fast."

As Blake turned, he saw a big luxury car moving too quickly for the safety of the nearby pedestrians. He looked around for Wren.

A couple of people called out, "Slow down!"

The driver did ease off on the speed. Good.

But where was Wren?

On the other side of the street, Zoey turned, her yellow dress swirling. Her expression changed from curiosity to horror. "No!" she cried, rushing forward.

The car skidded to a stop. There was an ugly *thump*.

He pushed through the surging, curious crowd. "Excuse me. Excuse me. I need to get through."

"Call 911," he heard Kelly say to Alec, her voice grim. She picked up Zinnia, who'd been playing beside her.

Wren wasn't with Zinnia. Oh, no.

Blake burst out of the crowd.

Zoey knelt in the middle of the street, right in front of the luxury car. Its doors were both open, and two people stood over Zoey. Carol Ann's parents.

As Blake reached them, he saw his worst nightmare.

Wren lay motionless on the ground.

An hour later, Zoey's heart was still in her throat. She gripped the door handle of Kelly's car as they pulled into the hospital parking lot.

In the chaos immediately after Wren had been hit, it had been hard to know what to do. Zoey had rushed to Wren, of course, as had several others including the driver of the vehicle that had hit her. The dear child lay motionless and unconscious on the ground. "Is there a doctor around?" someone had asked, and the call had been taken up by several people, louder.

Zoey had touched Wren's neck and felt a pulse, and another bystander had done the same thing. They'd looked at each other and nodded, and he'd called, "She's alive," just as Blake reached Wren and sank to his knees, his face white, running his hands gently over her legs and arms.

Church people had immediately surrounded the unconscious little girl, praying. A doctor had been found among the congregation and brought through the crowd. He'd looked her over and cautioned everyone to keep a distance and told Blake not to pick her up, even when she'd awakened, started to cry and extended one arm toward him.

The other arm was bent in a strange way.

Blake had sat on the ground beside Wren to wait for the EMTs, speaking calmly and quietly, stroking her hair, even making her smile a little.

The ambulance had arrived minutes after Wren had been hit. Once the EMTs had started working on Wren, several of Blake's guy friends had surrounded him, talking and praying quietly.

There had been another disturbance when Wren's grandfather, who'd been driving the car that had hit Wren, had sunk down onto the pavement, dizzy and struggling to breathe. The police officer who'd arrived to deal with the accident scene had checked him over and helped him to his feet.

The older man had waved away the offer of medical help. Wren had been taken to the hospital, Blake riding along.

When Kelly and Zoey had left, following several other family members and church friends, Carol Ann's parents had been sitting on a bench outside the church, answering questions from the officer. Karen had been crying.

Now, Kelly parked the car, crooked, and the two of them rushed into the hospital.

"It wasn't your fault," Kelly said, sounding out of breath.

"It *was* my fault. She was running after me."

"It was Blake's fault. He didn't keep ahold of his child. It was his parents' fault. They should have been watching her. And Carol Ann's dad! He has glaucoma. He shouldn't even be driving." Kelly steered her toward the information desk. "Where would they bring a little girl who's been in a car accident?" she asked the woman behind the desk.

The volunteer's forehead creased with sympathy. "If she was just brought in, she's probably in the ER. Unless they rushed her right into surgery." She pointed them toward a long hall and they hurried down it.

Amidst the antiseptic smells and quiet intercom announcements and elevator bells, a small cluster of people—Blake's parents, the pastor and Sharlene and her daughter—sat in the waiting room for the ER.

Zoey rushed to them. "How is she?"

The pastor stood. "The doctors think she has a concussion, but it's her arm they're most concerned about. Blake's with her, of course. And I'm about to use my clergy privilege and try to get in to see them." He walked toward the desk.

"One of the nurses came out and told us she's conscious and loving the attention," Sharlene said.

Zoey sank into a chair. "Thank you, Jesus."

Blake's mother scowled. "She was running after *you.*"

"I know she was," Zoey said. "I wish like anything I'd known it and stopped before crossing the street." The truth was, she'd been hurrying away from Blake and all the emotions he evoked.

Kelly sat down beside Zoey, put an arm around her and glared at Blake's mother. "It's not Zoey's fault," she said. "Everyone should have been keeping a better eye on her. Especially her father and her grandparents."

Sharlene had been talking quietly to her daughter, but now she came over to the small group of adults. "Hey, hey, now, we're all upset. Let's don't start throwing blame around. Let's just pray for that little girl."

So they all prayed, and then Kelly went for coffee, and Blake's parents talked quietly to each other. Sharlene's daughter started to cry and couldn't be consoled about her injured new friend, so Sharlene left after getting Zoey to promise to text her with any updates.

Carol Ann's parents came in, both subdued. They

sat across the room from the others, and then Karen came over to the group. "Is there any news?"

They shared what they knew. Pity twisted Zoey's heart. If she felt at fault, how must Carol Ann's father feel?

Blake and the pastor emerged, a doctor beside them, and everyone quieted down.

"She's going to be okay," Blake said, his face impossibly weary.

"We're about to take her into surgery," the doctor said. "Her arm is shattered, and it'll be delicate work to put it back together. You all should probably go home and rest up. Wren will be okay, but she has a long recovery in front of her. This man will need your support in the weeks ahead."

Across the waiting room, Carol Ann's father started to cry, his shoulders hunched and shaking. "I'm sorry, I'm so sorry," he choked out.

The pastor went to him and they sat side by side.

Blake walked over, squeezed Mr. Masterson's shoulder and then went to have a final word with the doctor. Everyone else started gathering their things.

"Do you want me to take you home?" Kelly asked Zoey.

"I'm not sure," Zoey said. She wanted to help Blake, but they were at odds. Still, Wren's health trumped everything. "Yes, take me home," she said slowly. "I think there's a way I can help."

Chapter Eight

Blake wiped a couple of remaining tears from Wren's face and pulled the covers up over her shoulders. Her even breathing didn't change. Good. Sleep was the best thing for her.

The hospital room was painted lavender, with a mural of a giraffe from floor to ceiling. Nice effort, but it couldn't negate the effect of the IV stand and beeping machines and disinfectant smell.

Nor of the bandage on the side of Wren's face and the giant cast encasing her arm.

His precious little girl could have died.

Blake sucked in a deep breath and let it out slowly, his face dropping into his hands. He thanked God once again for the quick-thinking EMTs and the skillful surgeon and the kind nurses who'd gotten Wren to the point of being safe.

Thanked God, too, for Wren's resilience. The pain hadn't phased her as much as the fact that she had to go to sleep without her ragged pink teddy bear. That was the reason for her tears. That, and her desire to see Zoey.

Blake blew out a sigh and prayed for wisdom. He needed a heaping portion of it to handle Wren's care and to figure out what to do about his, and Wren's, relationship with their beloved neighbor. Today had taught him that Wren's unrequited desire for Zoey to be her mother could be an actual danger.

"Mr. Evans?" A scrubs-clad doctor stood in the doorway, beckoning. "I wanted to touch base with you before I go off duty. Let's talk out here so your daughter can get the rest she needs."

Blake gave Wren one last pat on the leg. Her breathing had gotten slower and deeper, with the tiny snore that meant she was really out. Good. He headed into the hallway.

The pediatrics floor was quiet. Visiting hours were over, and most of the young patients were asleep. A couple of women stood outside a room at the end of the hall, talking quietly. A man in blue scrubs pushed a laundry cart past them, nodding a greeting to the doctor.

Blake had spoken briefly to the surgeon after the procedure, but hadn't gotten a lot of details. Or at least, he hadn't retained them. He admitted as much to this doctor. "Can you tell me any more about her prognosis?"

"She did very well in surgery," the doctor said. "We were able to put that shattered bone back together. I say we, but I only assisted. Dr. Clinton did the actual surgery. He's the best in the area."

"Thank you. I spoke with him, and he seemed positive about how things went. He said—I *think* he said—that she'd probably recover completely?"

"That's our hope and expectation. You can relax and take a snooze in the recliner in her room tonight, and then take her home tomorrow or the next day in all likelihood."

"So she'll be able to use the arm normally, once it heals?"

The doctor tilted a flat hand side to side. "Never any promises in my business, but I'd predict a full recovery. It's important that you keep it immobilized as it heals. Not an easy task with a child, but the cast will help a lot."

"Thank you. I appreciate what you've done for her, more than you know." Blake shook his head. "I can't believe I didn't watch her more closely. I turned my back for a minute, and she was running across the street."

"It happens all the time," the man said. "That's why we teach children to look both ways and keep them away from busy streets and use crossing guards. But all the efforts in the world don't stop a kid from being a kid."

Blake blew out a breath. "When I saw her lying in the street…" Tears threatened, and he swallowed hard. "I'm sorry. I'm sure you have work to do and patients to see."

The doctor patted Blake's shoulder, his expression kind. "Kids are resilient, more so than we are. Your daughter will be all right." He walked down the hall with a wave.

Blake checked on Wren, still sleeping soundly. Then he walked out to the waiting room.

Most of Blake's friends and family had gone home once they'd heard the surgeon's initial positive report.

His father was there, though, and Blake collapsed into the chair next to him.

"She's doing okay?" his father asked.

"Sleeping," Blake said. On the other side of the dimly lit room, a man and woman talked quietly. A television, muted, played a sitcom in one corner.

"Hungry?" his father asked. Without waiting for an answer, he handed Blake a sandwich wrapped in plastic and a container of cookies. From a cooler, he pulled out a bottle of water and handed it over.

Blake recognized the hearty whole-grain bread and the huge chocolate chip cookies. "Did Zoey bring these?"

Dad nodded. "She went home and got her car and brought food for anyone who needed it. I had to fight to save you a sandwich." He gave Blake a tired smile. "She brought a few things for you and Wren, too." He got a cloth bag off the seat beside him and set it on the floor beside Blake.

After another two bites of the thick turkey and cheese sandwich, Blake looked down into the bag. Pajamas for Wren, a phone charger and, tucked in one side, the crucial pink bear.

He felt a rush of gratitude. What kindness. "Where's Zoey now?"

"She had to go. Mom's walking her down to her car now." Dad's forehead furrowed. "So Zoey has a key to your house?"

Blake took another bite of sandwich and then wiped his mouth. "She knows where the spare key is, yes," he said.

Dad gave him a sideways glance. "She's a sweet girl," he said, "but…" He paused. "Just be careful. You wouldn't want Wren to go through another loss if things don't work out."

"No, I wouldn't." Blake was too emotionally drained to get into a discussion about Zoey. He finished his sandwich, balled up the wrapper and ate two cookies, one after the other.

Dad was right, of course, though maybe not for the reasons he meant.

Blake's father, being biased, thought Blake was worthy to marry the queen of England. Mom was even more that way. He was their only child, and they saw him as incredibly special.

Blake knew otherwise. He'd been no great shakes as a husband. And he wasn't the perfect dad, either. Not even close. After all, he'd let his beloved daughter get hit by a car today.

He knew he wasn't worthy of a woman like Zoey, but he was definitely grateful to have her as a friend. If he still did.

Zoey reached her car and turned to face Blake's mother. "You didn't have to walk me out, but thank you," she said. "I can drive you back to the entrance if you'd like." It wasn't far, but Mrs. Evans's normally neat hair was mussed and her eyes had deep circles beneath them. The woman had to be exhausted after this emotional day.

"I'll be fine." She waited while Zoey got into the car and opened the window. She leaned in. "You know, dear, that accident wouldn't have happened if you and Wren hadn't gotten so attached."

It was nothing more than Zoey had thought herself, but still, the words hit her like a physical blow.

"I know you didn't mean for it to happen. We're all at fault for not watching her. I just think…you should keep a little more distance. I could tell you hoped bringing food and Wren's things would endear you to Blake—"

"I just wanted to help," Zoey interrupted, forcing out the words through a tight throat.

"Of course. You're a sweet girl. It's just… Blake is too kind to tell you this, but he and Wren can't be the family you're looking for." She gave Zoey a stiff little smile, turned and trudged back toward the hospital entrance.

Zoey watched her go, closed the window and fought off a surge of resentment. *No good deed goes unpunished,* as Rena at the diner sometimes said. She'd just wanted to help, to do something kind for the family and for Blake and Wren.

She let her head drop back against the seat. Her chest felt as empty as it had when she'd been taken to her first foster home. Emptier.

Overhead, the moon cast a cold, silvery light.

Zoey felt cold, too. Chilled to the bone. Frozen out of the lives of the father and daughter who meant so much to her.

She swallowed hard and closed her eyes and prayed, a wordless prayer for help, solace, *something* to stop the aching of her heart.

* * *

Once she got home, she couldn't relax. It was nine o'clock and dark, but the spring evening was warm, and Holiday Point was a safe town. She put on her walking shoes and headed out, determined to exhaust herself and in that way, quiet the ugly voices in her head.

She'd walk, and pray, and maybe figure some things out.

Soon she was in the heart of town, walking briskly down the street. Streetlights shone overhead as she passed the shops, all closed now. A car passed on the cross street, and then a woman walking a tiny dog greeted her. Otherwise, it was quiet and she was alone.

Which was good. She didn't have to hide the few tears that rolled down her face.

Blake and Wren can't be the family you're looking for. Well, she'd known that. But Blake had become a good friend, really her best friend, and she relied on him a lot. For a short while, when he'd kissed her, she'd thought there might be more. Wanted there to be more.

But that was the mistake of getting her hopes up. She couldn't let that happen again.

Up ahead, a woman was fitting a key into the lock of a door that must lead to the apartments over the shops. She opened it and then glanced over. "Zoey? Is that you?"

Zoey slowed her steps, wiped her eyes and squinted at the woman. "Oh, Olivia, hi." Olivia was a friend of Zoey's friend Kelly, a nice woman who worked with the kids at church. She'd been Wren's preschool teacher. She and Zoey weren't close, but they were friendly.

"I'm guessing you know more than I do," Olivia said, "since you're friends with Blake and the family. How is Wren?"

"She had to have surgery on her arm, but she's doing well."

Olivia studied her. "How are *you* doing? That must have been pretty scary."

"It was awful. But…all's well that ends well."

Olivia raised a skeptical eyebrow. "Would you like to come up for a cup of tea? I have this delicious cinnamon and spice blend, and it's decaf."

"Uh…sure. That would be nice." Anything would be better than being alone with her thoughts.

They climbed the steps to Olivia's apartment. It was small, with old woodwork and big windows overlooking the town. Olivia gestured toward a couple of cozy chairs. "Sit down, and I'll fix us tea. You're not allergic to cats, are you?" As she said it, an orange tabby jumped into Zoey's lap.

"No, I like them," Zoey said, laughing as the creature pushed its head against her hand.

"He's not the typical standoffish cat," Olivia said. "Rusty is an attention hog."

Zoey sat and petted the cat while Olivia bustled around in the kitchen at the other end of the apartment's big main room. Moments later, she came over with two cups of tea and a little dish for the tea bags. She set them down and then brought out a bakery-style box of cookies and opened it. "Have one of Kelly's cookies. They'll cheer anyone up."

"Thanks." Zoey wasn't hungry, but she sipped the tea and then bit into an oatmeal raisin cookie. "You're right. This is delicious."

They munched for a minute, and then Olivia tucked her feet underneath herself. "I want to ask you something, but I shouldn't. I hate it when people assume my love life, or lack of it, is their business."

Zoey sighed. "People do tend to do that, when you're a single woman. What do you want to ask?" She was pretty sure she knew.

"Are you and Blake an item?"

"No." Zoey dunked her tea bag into her cup, over and over, and then put it into the little dish. "I thought we might be, at one point, but it's never going to happen."

Olivia didn't pry into reasons. "How is it living next door to him, then?" she asked instead.

Zoey thought about the easy back-and-forth she and Blake had enjoyed for the past couple of years. Drifting in and out of each other's houses, borrowing things, doing favors.

That wasn't going to happen anymore. Mrs. Evans had suggested Zoey keep more of a distance, which was annoying and interfering, but no more than Zoey had been thinking herself. "It's not good, being next-door neighbors. Not anymore. For me, or Blake, or Wren."

"Wren seems pretty attached to you," Olivia said.

She took another sip of tea. "Are you thinking of moving?"

Until this moment, Zoey hadn't been. But the thought of escaping all the tumultuous emotions of the past few days was the only thing that felt right. "I guess maybe I am."

"I'm not just being nosy. There's a vacancy next door," Olivia said. "I'd love to get a friendly neighbor in there. The last guy was a recluse who got mad when Rusty came out in the hall."

"Hmm." Zoey looked around, thinking. "It's next door?"

"Right over the knitting shop. It's almost exactly like this one." Olivia took another cookie. "Will you think about it?"

Zoey was more of a country person, liking the yard and the garden of the little cottage she was renting. Living above a shop would be completely different.

But Holiday Point wasn't exactly a metropolis. There was a big park just down the street.

And she needed a change.

She stroked the cat in her lap. She could be like Olivia, a strong single woman living in town. She'd be closer to the diner. She could get to know Olivia better. Take up knitting. Maybe get a cat.

As if on cue, Rusty started to purr.

The idea of moving away from Blake and Wren broke her heart, but it was what was best for Wren. And for Blake, and definitely for Zoey. "I'm interested," she said. "Can you give me your landlord's phone number?"

Chapter Nine

Blake had been warned that the third day after Wren's surgery would be the hardest. He'd thought he was prepared.

He wasn't.

Caring for a hurting five-year-old who had to stay quiet and still in bed was more challenging than the toughest calculus class he'd ever taught.

He kept reminding himself that Wren's surgery had gone well and she was going to be okay. He prayed an infinite number of prayers of thanksgiving for that. It truly put things in perspective.

He could have lost Wren. He could be grieving, planning a funeral like one of the families he'd met on the pediatric floor of the hospital.

He sent up a prayer for them, too, and made a note to donate to the pediatric cancer fund in little Rowan Anderson's name.

Wren called out fretfully from her bed. "Can I get up *now*, Daddy?"

He sighed. Her nap had lasted only half an hour, which made sense; the poor kid hadn't had any fresh air or physical activity since Sunday.

He went into her room. "How's my one-armed princess feeling?"

She didn't smile. Instead, a big tear rolled down her face. "It hurts."

His heart squeezed inside him. "I know it does, baby. A lot or a little?"

"A lot," she said, her voice weak. "Can you make it stop?"

Blake hated that she had to learn at age five that daddies couldn't fix everything. Of course, she'd had an earlier lesson in that reality when Carol Ann had died, but she was too little to remember that. Her confidence in him had regrown, only to be cut down again.

"Let's go in the kitchen," he said. "You'll have to sit still at the table in the special chair Grammy fixed up yesterday, but you can watch me cook lunch and keep me company."

"Can I have a cookie?" she asked.

"After lunch." Carefully, he pulled back her covers and helped her to her feet. She winced, which made Blake wince, too.

He walked beside her, encouraging her to go slowly. She didn't protest too much. He could tell that every movement hurt. In the kitchen, he boosted her up into the armchair his mom had put there and propped her cast-clad arm onto the system of pillows they'd rigged up. He gave her a dose of the over-the-counter pain medicine the doctors had okayed for her to take in between the stronger meds.

"Grammy left us a chicken and rice casserole," he said. "I can heat that up, or we can have scrambled eggs."

She made a face. "Not hungry."

"It's important that you eat good food to make your

arm better," he said. He opened the refrigerator. "Yo-gurt? Cheese and crackers?"

"Yogurt," she said. "Strawberry."

He rummaged around and pulled out a container, relieved he had the flavor she craved today. It was the drinkable kind, so he got her some crackers, too. He peeled a banana to complete the meal. Not the best lunch, but not the worst. He heated up some of his mother's casserole for himself.

Thankfully, his parents had been here all day yes-terday, making it possible for Blake to complete his end-of-term reports. They'd offered to come again today, but he'd declined, and he could tell they were a little relieved. Dad had to go to work, and Mom was in charge of the spring rummage sale at church. Blake was off now, until summer school started. He needed to take care of Wren himself.

He glanced out the window as he waited for the mi-crowave to ding. Normally, Zoey would be over here in a situation like this. Last year when Wren had been sick, she'd come over every day. Not that he'd expected Zoey to do the dirty work or wait on Wren. It was more about the company, both for Wren and for him.

He wanted to call her, picked up his phone to do it, and then set it back down on the table. No. He'd hurt her, pushed her away after that magnificent kiss. She'd literally been walking away from him when all this had happened.

But she'd come to the hospital and brought sand-wiches and cookies and the things they needed. Maybe she still cared about them. Maybe they could still be friends. He dug into his food, thinking about it, hoping it was so. He encouraged Wren to eat more of her lunch.

"I ate. I get cookies now." Her lower lip stuck out.

"One cookie," he said and then gave her two.

He pulled out a couple of puzzles and sat next to her at the table, pretending to find them difficult. They played Chutes and Ladders. They looked out the window at the rain.

Of course, looking out the window made Blake think more about Zoey. What was her schedule? Was she at work now? He was pretty sure she worked the breakfast and lunch shift on Wednesday. Maybe she'd come over afterward.

The thought lifted his spirits. He'd been a jerk to her and he knew it. He'd apologize when she came over, and they'd get back to their normal friendship.

No more kissing, he reminded himself. Arm's length.

Arm's length was better than entirely out of sight.

"I'm bored," Wren announced.

Of course she was. So was he. He gave in to the inevitable and set her up in front of the television, with reminders to stay put and keep her arm still and call him for anything she needed. Then he went back to the kitchen, grabbed a thriller he'd been reading before the accident and tried to get back into it.

No use. He checked on Wren and then dug out a book he thought of as a cheater's Bible. It had verses for all kinds of situations, alphabetically arranged. Anxiety. Boredom. Cancer. Doubt.

He'd just flipped to the parenting section when he heard a car with a bad muffler pull up. His heart leaped. Zoey's car.

Wren rushed in from the living room.

"Honey, you're not supposed to move around," he said, going to her. Gently, he picked her up.

"I was careful. Wanna see Zoey."

So did he. "She may be busy," he warned Wren, not wanting to get her hopes up. Holding her, he looked out the window.

Zoey *was* busy.

She was carrying a big load of flattened boxes into her house, her head bowed against the rain.

Why did she have boxes? They almost looked like...

Moving boxes.

He got a sinking feeling.

"Want Zoey," Wren said fretfully.

"Not right now."

Wren wound up for a full-fledged tantrum. He wasn't going to be able to keep her arm still if she melted down. She could reinjure herself.

"Come on. Let's go back in the living room. You can watch the kids' cartoons channel." That was a rare thing for Wren, who was usually limited to educational shows.

"No!" she wailed. "Don't wanna watch TV!"

He carried her into the living room and pulled out that last tool in his toolbox. "Here. You can play on my phone."

Her tears dried instantly. "Okay!"

He showed her where a few kids' games were located and handed it over. She hadn't really needed the instruction; somehow she, like other kids her age, was already comfortable with technology. She started playing a game involving a fox and was soon engrossed.

Leaving Blake free to deal with the sick, empty feeling that rose up in his chest at the thought of Zoey, his best friend, moving away.

Zoey opened and taped three big boxes and carried them upstairs.

She'd viewed the apartment next to Olivia's yesterday and told the landlord she was very interested.

After her breakfast-and-lunch shift, she'd picked up spare moving boxes from Rena, her boss, who'd moved here not too long ago. Rena kindly didn't ask a lot of questions once she was reassured Zoey would stay in the area and keep working for her at the diner.

Today, as a start, Zoey was going to pack up all the junk she'd stored in the cottage's spare bedroom. She wouldn't have space for it in the new place, but there was a lot that could go to the church rummage sale, conveniently scheduled for the next weekend.

She opened the closet and started pulling out clothes. High school jeans she'd never wear again. A fancy dress from the one dance she'd gone to back in eleventh grade, a hand-me-down from Carol Ann that had required her to safety-pin the bodice and pack tissues into her bra.

She folded it into the box, looked heavenward and thanked God for the woman who had handed down her old clothes and had gotten Zoey through high school with grades good enough to graduate.

Carol Ann had been a believer and was with Jesus now. Zoey was sure that she was loving Wren from heaven.

She looked in the direction of Blake's house. How was Wren doing? How was Blake?

It wasn't her business. It really wasn't. She needed to focus on the future rather than the past.

True, she hadn't been able to resist bringing home a lunch special for Blake and a big container of the buttered noodles Wren loved. She'd put them on their porch later, along with the small gift she'd picked up for Wren. No contact needed.

Focus on yourself, not on them.

Realizing she should save the good boxes for packing up the kitchen, Zoey got a container of large garbage bags from under her kitchen sink and brought them upstairs. She started stuffing the oldest clothes into them. Unfortunately, that called to mind the way she'd had to pack her things into garbage bags to move to the foster home in Holiday Point. That had been a miserable and scary day as she'd anticipated a new family, new town and new school, all totally unfamiliar.

She blew out a disgusted sigh. Why did the past keep rising up in her mind?

Her phone vibrated. Good. She'd escape the hard memories. She pulled it out, looked at the screen… and her heart gave a big jump and then started pounding steadily. Blake.

She'd probably fielded hundreds of calls from him over the years. She'd never had a reaction like this.

She accepted the call. "Hi, Blake."

Instead of his deep voice, a faint little-girl voice spoke. "Can you come over?"

"Wren? Are you okay?"

The little girl giggled. "Daddy said I could play with his phone, so I played!"

Oh, brother. Chuckling, Zoey said, "Take the phone to Daddy." Or wait, was Wren even supposed to be moving around the house? "Honey, just ask Dad to—"

"Wren? Are you talking to somebody or just pretending?" Blake's voice came through, faintly.

"I called Zoey, and she's coming over!"

"Give me the phone." A moment later, his voice got much clearer. "Zoey? Are you there?"

"Yes, it's me. Wren figured out how to call me on your phone."

She heard him sigh. "Did you tell her you'd come over?"

"No. We hadn't gotten that far. She made the assumption I would, though."

"We would love some company, but if you're too busy or don't want to, it's okay."

Zoey hesitated. It was probably better for all of them if she kept her distance. On the other hand, she'd brought home food for them.

And she did have something she wanted to say to Blake. Might as well get it over with.

"I'll come for a quick visit," she said and ended the call.

As soon as Blake opened the door, Zoey was glad she'd come. "You look awful," she said. His eyes had bags beneath them, and he hadn't shaved. His shirt had a stain on one shoulder. Purple, probably grape jam or juice.

"I've had better days," he admitted. "Come on in. Wren promised she'd stay quiet and keep her arm still if you came over."

Wren was creeping up behind him, holding her finger to her lips.

A cast covered her arm from shoulder to wrist. It looked huge on her, and Zoey's throat tightened. She put the food she'd brought on the table and knelt down. "Hi, honey," she said. "Let's have a quick, gentle hug and then you can get back to wherever you're supposed to be resting."

She folded the little girl into her arms and buried her face in her hair. *Thank You, God, for keeping this sweet child safe.* She blinked back tears. "Somebody needs a shampoo," she joked.

Wren giggled. "Daddy says I'm gonna have a bath tonight with a big bag on my arm!"

"I brought you all some food from the diner," she said, looking up at Blake. "Want me to put it in the fridge?"

"That would be great. Thank you. And thank you for the sandwiches and cookies at the hospital."

"Glad to help." Her well-intended gift hadn't sat as well with his mother as it apparently had with Blake, but he didn't need to know that.

They followed her into the kitchen, and Blake helped

Wren into her chair and steadied her arm on pillows while Zoey put away the food. Then she handed the bag she'd brought to Wren. "This is for you."

Wren dug through the bag of glitter crayons and colorful stickers and construction paper with her good hand, squealing with delight.

"Thank you, but you didn't have to spend your money on us," Blake said.

"Dollar store. I figured she'd like some new entertainment."

He nodded. "You were right. She's gotten bored with her usual toys and books already."

It felt awkward, keeping their discussion on the surface like this. But it was easier than talking about complicated feelings. "I can color with you for a little while," she told Wren and sat down across from her.

Within half an hour, Wren had slowed down. Her forehead wrinkled. "It hurts, Daddy," she said. "It really hurts."

Blake glanced at the old-fashioned kitchen clock. "Time for the strong meds," he said. "And then you can have a little rest."

He gave her some liquid medication, and within a few minutes, her eyes started to close. It was a mark of how not recovered she was that she didn't protest being carried to bed. "Zoey come," she said.

So Zoey did. Maybe it was wrong, but she wanted to comfort this sweet child who was the closest thing to a daughter she would probably ever have. While Blake straightened up the bedroom, Zoey sat on the edge of the bed and stroked Wren's good arm and sang a simple song she knew Wren loved.

Thankfully, by the time her throat closed up, Wren was asleep.

Zoey sat for another minute, studying Wren's dear face, so calm and pretty in repose. It was going to be so hard to leave this child's life.

But, according to Blake's mom, Zoey was hurting her by being a part of it.

She was probably right.

For Zoey to be as close to Blake and Wren as she'd been, it was no wonder Wren had started to think of her as a mother. She needed to get out of the way. Let Blake find someone else, someone more suitable for the long term.

"I think she's out," Blake said from the doorway.

She followed him to the kitchen. Should she tell him what was going on or just run away like a scared rabbit?

"Cup of tea?" he asked, holding up a tin of her favorite peppermint blend. She'd brought it over months ago so she wouldn't have to keep running to her house to get a tea bag.

"Uh, sure." How many of her things were in his house? They'd gotten so intertwined. She'd have to ask him to pack up a box of her stuff and leave it on her porch.

It felt horribly like a breakup.

Stop being so dramatic. She watched him microwave the water and plunk a tea bag in it, then pour himself a cup of coffee.

Time to say what needed to be said. "Listen," she said, "I want to apologize to you for my role in that accident," she said. "I feel awful about it."

His eyebrows drew together, and he shook his head. "You're the least responsible of any of us."

"That's not what your mom thinks," she blurted out.

He stared. "What did Mom say to you?"

"She told me it would never have happened if Wren hadn't gotten so attached and run after me. Which is true."

"Oh, Zoey. I'm sorry she said that. She's wrong to blame you." He sighed. "I should have been watching Wren much more closely. Mom and Dad should have kept an eye on her, too. And Carol Ann's dad should never have been driving."

She was glad to know that Blake, at least, didn't hold her responsible for what had happened. "How are Carol Ann's folks doing?" she asked. "They were pretty broken up at the hospital."

"They're…humbled, I guess is what you would say. He turned in his driver's license. And of course, I won't sue them. But they're conscious of what a mistake they made and the consequences it could have had." He pointed to an enormous stuffed horse parked in the corner of the room. "They sent that over. It moves and whinnies, and Wren can ride it."

Zoey winced. "Not right now, though, right?"

"Right. Not the best timing. If she fell off, she could reinjure her arm."

Zoey sipped tea and then started straightening art supplies on the table, suddenly nervous.

Blake looked at her over the rim of his own cup. "I have to ask," he said finally. "I saw out the window that you brought home boxes. How come?"

Zoey cleared her throat. She had to tell him, and it might as well be now. Maybe he'd be glad, relieved. His parents certainly would be, and Carol Ann's parents, too. "I hope to move at the end of the month."

"That's what I was afraid of. Is it because of…?" He trailed off, then gestured to his own chest, then her, then back to himself. "Is it because of what's been going on between us?"

She took another sip of tea to loosen her tight throat. "This isn't good for us, Blake. Not for me, not for you, and especially not for Wren."

He opened his mouth as if to protest and then shut it again. Emotions she couldn't decipher flickered across his handsome face.

She needed to stop seeing him as handsome. Needed to stop seeing him at all. "I'd better go," she said abruptly and stood.

"Moving seems so drastic. Stay for a little bit. We should talk about this."

She reached the door and put on her coat.

"Wait. Do you have a plan of where to go?" He followed her, his hand outstretched.

If he touched her, she couldn't bear the pain of leaving. "I won't be that far. Really. It'll be fine. You'll hardly notice I'm gone." And she fled out into the rain, running away.

Chapter Ten

On Friday afternoon, Blake opened his door to an entourage. Cam, Cam's brother Alec, Alec's daughter, Zinnia, and their therapy dog, Pokey. He'd known they were coming, because they'd called first, but the effect was still overwhelming.

And thrilling to Wren, who'd been out of sorts since lunchtime and lonely for days. "Pokey!" she shrieked, jumping off the couch. "Zinnia!"

Blake put a hand on Wren's good shoulder. "Careful. No hugs."

At the same moment, Alec knelt beside Zinnia. "Remember what we talked about. Quiet play, and no running or touching."

"Okay, Daddy," both girls chorused in unison. Then they looked at each other and giggled.

Which meant they weren't taking the instructions all too seriously.

"Have a seat," Blake said to his friends. "Girls, you can play here or in the kitchen." He figured he'd be able to keep an eye on them better out here than back in Wren's bedroom. "Drinks?" he asked Alec and Cam.

"Brought our own." Cam held up a cooler. "And Jodi sent homemade mac and cheese you can stick in the oven for later. She's sorry she couldn't come."

"Kelly's over visiting with Zoey," Alec said.

She was? What were they talking about? Blake forced his mind away from what might be going on next door. "Thanks for the food. My cooking skills aren't up to meal after meal at home." Normally, they'd have eaten at the diner at least every couple of days, but that was too much activity for Wren. Besides, he'd been trying not to come into too much contact with Zoey, who clearly wanted to avoid him. He took the casserole dish and put it into the refrigerator.

Back in the living room, Cam was pulling out cans of soda. "How are you holding up?" he asked.

"It's been rough." Blake sank back into his chair, suddenly realizing how exhausted he was. "Wren's feeling better, but she's not cleared for school yet. When all of her friends are in school, it makes for long days."

"I couldn't have my friend Boris over after school," Wren called from where she was petting the ever-patient Pokey. "'Cause he's too active."

"I know Boris," Zinnia said. "He's w-i-i-ld!"

Wren rose to her knees. "And yesterday Grandmother and Grandpa brought kittens, and Daddy wouldn't let me keep them!"

Cam's eyes widened, and Alec stifled a laugh. "Maybe now's not the time for a new pet," he said tactfully.

That was an understatement. Blake had been stunned to open the door and find his mother-in-law holding a basket with two small but very active kittens in it. "Grandmother and Grandpa are keeping them for now, and we can visit once the doctor says it's okay to move around. You have to rest and get better first."

Wren rolled her eyes, looking for all the world like a tiny teenager. Then she flopped down beside Pokey again.

"Was it your folks or Carol Ann's who brought the kittens?" Alec asked in a low voice.

"Carol Ann's," Blake said. "They feel so awful about what happened. They're trying to make it better."

"Grandmother cried," Wren announced.

So they weren't going to be able to have a conversation separate from the girls. That was okay. Blake didn't necessarily want to tell his friends about the biggest source of despair for him: Zoey's impending move.

He'd tried not to be all creepy, looking out the window to see what she was doing. Twice, though, he'd seen her carrying boxes and bags to her car.

Maybe it was just the fact that he was exhausted and upset from what had happened to Wren, but to him, Zoey's moving away seemed like the end of the world.

Cam and Alec glanced at each other. "How about if I stay here and supervise the girls and Pokey?" Alec said. "The two of you can take a walk or sit outside. I'm guessing an hour off duty would do you a world of good."

"You don't have to ask me twice," Blake said, standing. He went over to Wren. "You stay here and play with Zinnia and Pokey," he said. "I'll be out on the deck, and Zinnia's dad will be here if you need any-thing."

"Okay, Daddy." She looked up at him happily. "Pokey likes me!"

"Of course she does," he said and gave his daughter a kiss on the top of her head. Love expanded in him, so much he could barely restrain the impulse to wrap his daughter in a bear hug. This whole experience had made him incredibly emotional, but he didn't want to frighten Wren with his anxiety and intensity.

In the kitchen, he rummaged around until he found a bag of kids' crackers shaped like dogs and cats. He poured some into a bowl for the girls and Alec, and some into a bowl for him and Cam. "Sorry I don't have anything better to offer a guest," he said to Cam. "Let's sit out on the deck."

The sun shone on Blake's face, warming him as he gestured Cam to a chair and sat beside him. The breeze was cool, and he could see the river through the flowering fruit trees that lined the back of the yard. Flanking the deck were two lilac bushes Carol Ann had planted. They still had enough blooms to send out a sweet fragrance.

"Nice out here," Cam commented.

"It is. I haven't been able to get out much. Wren wants to run and play when she comes out, and she has to keep her arm steady until we see the doctor again. So we've stayed mostly inside."

"Must be rough to keep a kid quiet at that age.

That's why I didn't bring my boys over. They're a little too rowdy as playmates right now."

"Glad Alec thought of bringing Pokey." Trained as a therapy dog, Pokey was a sweet, calm dog who was accustomed to children. She'd visited in Wren's preschool and kindergarten classrooms. All the kids loved her, and Blake was familiar enough with the dog to be perfectly comfortable leaving Wren in her company. Unlike the kittens. Yes, they'd been adorable, but they'd run wildly through the house, scratched Wren with their tiny claws and gotten stuck behind the refrigerator, causing Wren to have a meltdown. Even Carol Ann's parents had quickly realized that this wasn't the best time for kittens.

Blake sipped his drink and sat in comfortable silence with his friend. Comfortable until the sound of women's laughter from next door made both of them look toward Zoey's house.

"How are things between the two of you?" Cam asked, nodding sideways toward Zoey's house.

Blake shook his head. "Things are nowhere. Even our friendship has fallen off."

"Oh?" Cam looked at him with interest. "What happened?"

Blake blew out a sigh. He really wasn't one to talk about his problems, but keeping them to himself wasn't doing him a whole lot of good.

He'd prayed for guidance. Maybe God had sent Cam to offer it. "We started getting closer," Blake admitted. "But that's just not the right thing for me to do. I backed off and it hurt her."

"How come it's not the right thing for you?"

Blake spread his hands and shrugged. "I'm bad at marriage, and I'm also not the type to toy with a woman, go short-term. Especially someone like Zoey." He thought about her smiling face, her trusting eyes. No, he couldn't explore a relationship with her when the likelihood was that he'd ruin it.

"What makes you think you're bad at marriage? Your wife?"

Blake nodded. "I couldn't make her happy. I was thoughtless, didn't give her the space she needed. Didn't know how to show her a good time, I guess. I wasn't fun."

"That stuff doesn't always come naturally," Cam said, his voice mild. "Might be you would've done better if you'd had the time to grow up. I for sure had to grow up, get my temper and my jealousy under control before I could be a fit husband for Jodi."

"We'd made the decision to go to counseling, but she died before we could have the first appointment." Blake blurted out the words he'd barely said to anyone. He had a sudden memory of the counselor's scheduling service calling, asking in a faintly accusatory voice why they'd missed their appointment. Blake hadn't had the energy to soften his answer. "She died," he had said abruptly and hung up. "Counselor sent us a bill because we hadn't canceled the session." He was still a little bit bitter.

Cam shook his head. "People are awful sometimes. Did you pay it?"

Blake frowned, trying to remember. "I think I did.

I was on autopilot. Didn't have energy to question or fight anything."

"Must've been a rough time." Cam crunched into a cracker. "Hey, these aren't too bad."

"I buy them for myself as much as for Wren," Blake admitted.

They sat for a few minutes, quiet. A pair of squirrels chased each other across the lawn and up the big oak tree. On the river, Blake made out the tiny figures of two fishermen in a rowboat, their voices amplified across the water when one of them caught something.

"I felt pretty guilty when my wife left," Cam said suddenly.

Blake raised an eyebrow. He'd heard stories. "Why did you feel guilty when it was her who left?"

Cam let out a humorless laugh. "At first I was just mad, believe me. Mad for the sake of my sons. They're still dealing with the effects of it, though getting better all the time."

Blake nodded, thinking of Cam's lively, happy boys. It was good to have examples of how resilient kids could be. He hoped Wren would get less and less affected by her grief, that it would settle into a few good memories of being deeply loved by her mother.

"Late at night," Cam went on, "I'd get to thinking, facing facts. I wasn't the best husband in the world. Left my wife alone too much. Didn't do my share around the house. Didn't take her out dancing like I did when we were dating." His mouth twisted into a half smile. "Believe me, I still put more blame on her than me, especially in how she did it, leaving the boys alone. But I felt the guilt about being a bad husband, and for a while, I didn't think I'd ever find love again."

Funny that Cam had dealt with feeling inadequate as a husband, too. "You and Jodi seem to have a great relationship."

"We do," Cam said. "We work on it and pray about it, and I pay a lot more attention than I did the first time around. That's kinda the point, brother. You might not have been husband of the year before, but there's hope. God gives second chances."

Was that true? Could he try again at love, even though he'd failed so miserably the first time around?

A truck pulled into the driveway that separated Zoey's house from Blake's. A man got out, just as Kelly and Zoey emerged, both carrying boxes. The man hustled over and took both boxes, carrying them easily to the truck and putting them in the bed.

Then he caught up with Zoey and Kelly, who'd turned to go back into the house. He said something that made all three of them laugh.

The sound stabbed Blake in the heart.

Maybe God did give second chances, but it was questionable whether he was eligible for one. Maybe he didn't have it in him to do better on a second try. Or maybe he'd just waited too long to make his move.

Zoey leaned back against the headrest of Geoff's truck and sighed. "So good to get all of that stuff out of my place. Thank you both, so much. Geoff, I could never have done it without a truck."

"Yes, you're the best." Kelly, who'd suggested him as a driver and was now sitting in between him and Zoey, patted his arm. Geoff was a custodian at the school and came into the diner often. He was also a faithful believer who was always willing to lend a hand or a truck to help others.

Why couldn't Zoey have fallen for a younger version of Geoff?

The sun hung low in the sky, casting a golden light over the homes and yards of Holiday Point. Through the truck's open windows, the fragrance of fresh spring grass drifted in, along with the sound of a lawn mower.

The truck bounced over a pothole, causing her and Kelly to bob in their seats.

"Sorry about that," Geoff said. "I'm glad to help out, but I never promised good shocks."

"No worse than mine," Zoey said, laughing. "I'm just relieved to get this junk to the rummage sale. It'll benefit someone else and make a little money for the church."

And hopefully, donating her old things would help her let go of the past.

Even the thought of Blake and Wren being a part of her past made Zoey's heart ache. She wanted to know how they were doing. Wanted to stop by and see Wren, help with her care.

But it wouldn't go anywhere. She had to make room for Blake to have someone else, someone more appropriate, in his life. Had to make room in her own life for love, too, and that meant she couldn't live next door to the man she'd fallen for.

"Purging your stuff can be cathartic," Geoff said.

"It can. It always is on the reality shows," Kelly said. "Moving can be cathartic, too."

Kelly would know, Zoey thought. She'd heard the story of how Kelly had been house-sitting over the holidays in preparation for moving out of her parents' place. Alec had ended up at the same house through a misunderstanding with his daughter, Zinnia, during a snowstorm. Somehow their chance relationship had evolved into a beautiful marriage. Kelly was every bit a mother to Zinnia.

Zoey longed for that herself. "I'm hoping it'll be cathartic to move away from the guy I've been in unrequited love with for too long," she blurted out, surprising herself. But Kelly knew all about it, and Geoff was so friendly and accepting, and almost old enough to be a father figure.

He lifted an eyebrow. "So you fell for the dude next door?"

Zoey thought about Blake. His dear face, his hearty laugh, his love for his daughter. "I guess I did," she said.

"Let me ask you this," Geoff said. "Did he take you out?"

"Like on a date?" She shook her head. "No. We're friends. *Were* friends," she amended. She had to start thinking that way. Had to put their relationship into the past, mentally *and* physically, before her heart would follow suit.

Geoff nodded. "The trouble with those friend-first relationships is, you can end up taking each other for granted. Too buddy-buddy, not romantic enough. Where he doesn't have to try very hard."

Zoey glanced at Kelly, who looked surprised. Then they both looked at Geoff. "Is that the voice of experience?" Kelly asked.

Beneath his dark beard, Geoff reddened. "Kind of," he said.

"Sounds like a story," Zoey said.

He gunned the motor as they passed through Holiday Point's only stoplight. "For another day."

"We'll hold you to that," Kelly said. Then she turned toward Zoey. "I think you and Blake could be great together," she said. "Friends, sure, that's a great start. But I could definitely see more."

Zoey shook her head. "He's a professor. I'm a waitress. I'd just bring him down."

Geoff hit the brakes, and the truck jolted to a stop in front of the park.

"What's wrong?" Zoey asked.

Geoff turned off the vehicle and faced her. "Does your profession determine your value?"

"Noooo." Zoey wondered if she'd insulted Geoff, who also worked in a less prestigious job, being a custodian. "But to Blake's parents, and to his late wife Carol Ann's parents, it does. They've both warned him, and me, against a relationship."

Kelly frowned. "Has Blake ever acted like a waitress isn't good enough for him?"

"No!" The idea was shocking. "He'd never do that."

"Of course not," Geoff said. "He's a Christian man. Don't forget that all the disciples had ordinary jobs. Mostly fishermen, and even a tax collector."

"Good point," Kelly said. "And the Pharisees had tons of education, but Jesus didn't value them more."

"Their jobs weren't important. Neither is yours, or Blake's. It's what's in your heart. Got it?" Geoff softened his words with a smile.

"Got it." She gave him a little salute, and he started the truck.

As they bounced and jolted toward home, Zoey thought about it.

She'd always felt that she wasn't intelligent enough for Blake, but it was true that he'd never made her feel less smart than he was. In some ways, like cooking and housework and understanding other people, she was smarter.

But it didn't matter, not really. The problem between them was that Blake didn't want a relationship with her. He'd shut her down.

As they pulled into the driveway, the sun sank below the trees, casting a filtered glow over the yards and the river.

And there, in the golden light, was Blake. He must have been waiting for them. He came out into the driveway and waved them down.

They climbed out and hurried over. "Is everything okay?" Kelly asked.

"Yes. I didn't mean to scare you. The kids are inside with Alec."

"Okay?" Kelly raised an eyebrow as if she were trying to read the situation. "I'll go in and see how they're doing. Geoff, want to come meet my daughter and our therapy dog?"

His smile was conspiratorial. "Sure thing."

They were leaving her alone with Blake.

He turned to her. "Can we talk for a few minutes?"

His face was so dear. She wanted to keep looking at it, wanted to hear what he had to say. But she thought about Geoff's comments.

She wasn't beneath Blake just because she was a waitress. And she deserved good treatment even though they were longtime friends.

"I'm tired right now," she said. *And you never took me out on a date.* "So no, I can't."

He looked surprised.

Had he expected she'd just roll over and come back when he whistled? From his deflated expression, it seemed that he had.

"Take care, Blake," she said. Then she turned and hurried into her house before she could give in.

* * *

After a week of almost no contact, Blake managed to talk Zoey into coming to the Memorial Day parade with him and Wren.

They walked the three blocks to the parade route, greeting neighbors and friends. Wren chattered enough to conceal the awkwardness between Blake and Zoey.

"Nice day for a parade," he said to break the silence.

"It is." She paused, then said, "It looks like Wren's feeling a lot better."

"She is. Her cast has made her a celebrity at school."

"That's good."

More silence. They were approaching the crowd lining Main Street. Everyone else was looking down the block, waiting for the parade, so there were no distractions from friends.

Blake's heart felt like a giant rock in his chest. When had things gotten so uncomfortable between him and Zoey? What had happened to their friendship?

Was it even worth asking what he wanted to ask her?

When Wren spotted Zinnia and ran ahead to see her, Zoey touched Blake's arm. "I came with you today for a reason," she said. "We need to tell Wren that I'm moving."

Her words threatened to crush his natural optimism, but he pushed forward with his own agenda. "I want to talk with you first."

She sighed. "This is hard for me, Blake. Don't make it harder."

In the distance, a shout went up, and the crowd's excitement got louder. The high school band started playing a ragged version of "Some Gave All."

Wren ran back to them. "Can I go watch the parade with Zinnia and Pokey?"

"Let me go talk to Zinnia's mom and dad." He looked at Zoey. "Wait here?"

"Sure," she said with a little frown.

He walked with Wren to the area where Kelly and Alec had snagged a bench. "Okay if Wren hangs with you for a bit?"

"Of course! We'd love to have her watch the parade with us."

"Thank you." Blake didn't feel too bad about asking, because he'd watched Zinnia last Saturday so that Kelly and Alec could have a night out. Now he leaned closer to the couple. "I could use your prayers for a talk I'm about to have with Zoey."

"You got it." Alec clapped him on the back. Kelly nodded, smiling.

Zoey wasn't smiling when Blake returned to her side. "I came today so we could talk to Wren," she said.

Tonya Mitford, a gossipy acquaintance, looked over at them, her expression curious.

"I wanted you to come for another reason," he said quietly. "Do you mind heading over where it's quieter?"

She looked at him, then at the approaching band, then at Tonya. "Okay, sure," she said without enthusiasm.

This was looking to be an uphill battle.

He led the way to a bench in the park, under a maple tree and blocked off on one side by a line of scraggly bushes. "Sit down," he said and waited for her to sit before joining her, a respectable couple of feet away. "Zoey, I..." He looked into her eyes then and realized just how important this moment was. For a long moment, he was tongue-tied.

"Lose your train of thought?" she asked finally.

"No, my nerve." He paused, then said, "I want to date you."

That was smooth.

Zoey stared at him for a moment and then spoke. "Where did this come from?"

"It's been growing a long time," he said. Overhead, a songbird trilled to its mate. Behind them, the sound of the crowd and the music blurred into background noise. "I've always cared for you, for a lot of reasons."

She looked intently into his eyes but didn't speak.

"After Carol Ann died, I needed a friend, badly, and you were there."

"I... I care for you, too, Blake, but—"

"It's grown, Zoey," he said, interrupting her before she could shut him down. "My feelings have grown into, well, into love."

She stared at him, opened her mouth as if to say something, closed it again.

He wanted so badly to touch her, to smooth back that strand of hair that kept blowing into her eyes, to hold her hand. But that might prompt a rejection he couldn't come back from. Desperate, he kept talking. "Kissing you was…well, it was great. I can't stop thinking about it." Was that too much emphasis on the physical? "Just being with you, day to day, it feels like sunshine. Seeing you with Wren—"

"Do you just want a mother for Wren?" she broke in.

"What?" Her words shocked him. "No! That wouldn't be a good reason for us to be together. I'm thrilled that you and Wren are close, but this is about you and me." He sucked in a breath and summed up, just as he would a lecture at the university. "Bottom line, I want to pursue a relationship with you."

She bit her lip, her face troubled. "I'm not your type, though, am I?"

"You're so much my type." He paused, watching the river as it flowed over the rocks. He tried to absorb its calm wisdom. "Look, I know Carol Ann's mom said some things. Maybe my parents did, too. Society puts a professor over a waitress, but you and I both know that's superficial stuff."

"You said it wouldn't work between us, though. You pushed me away."

"I did, and I'm sorry. I thought I couldn't be a decent husband, and I didn't want to inflict myself on you, but—"

"Oh, Blake." She shook her head, smiling. "For a smart guy, you have some not-so-bright ideas."

There was a shout of laughter from the parade behind them, and they both turned in time to see that a juggling clown was entertaining the crowd.

He dared to touch her hand. "I'm working on myself, and, well, God's working on me, too. Enough that I think we could be good together, Zoey. Do you care for me at all, enough to let me court you and try to win your heart?"

She hesitated. "I care for you," she said finally. There was something in her eyes, a light that hadn't been there before.

But he didn't want to presume. "As a friend, or more?" he asked.

"More. Maybe. I think." Her cheeks went pink. "This is all new to me."

He lifted her hand and kissed it. "That's okay," he said. "We can take it slow." He kissed each fingertip. "Or not."

"Blake!" But she was smiling.

His insides seemed ready to explode with the joy he felt. He glanced upward and breathed a *thank You*.

Finally, he brushed back that strand of hair that had blown, again, across her face. "Then…can I say that…we're dating?"

She lifted an eyebrow. "Are you going to take me on dates?"

"Yes!" The thought of actually dating Zoey made his heart swell with happiness. "We can go to shows, and movies, and that new restaurant over in Union-town. Whatever you want."

"That sounds wonderful, Blake." She squeezed his hand.

"Are you still going to move away?"

"I don't know." She frowned. "It might be good for me to do that. I just don't know."

"We can think about it. Work it out, together. Does that sound okay?"

She nodded. Her eyes flickered to his lips.

That was all the encouragement he needed. He pulled her close and kissed her, letting all his tenderness show for the first time.

It felt glorious and exciting and entirely, completely right.

Minutes later, a high-pitched voice broke through their romantic haze. "Look, Zinnia! Daddy's kissing Zoey!"

Blake and Zoey pulled back from each other and laughed, and Blake held out an arm as Zoey beckoned to Wren. She ran to them, and they pulled her into a wonderful group hug.

Holding Wren and Zoey, Blake closed his eyes as gratitude filled his heart to overflowing.

Epilogue

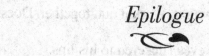

It was the Fourth of July, and Holiday Point was doing what it did on most holidays: gathering the community together.

Zoey's feelings were mixed.

Mostly, she was happy to be walking into the community cookout on Blake's arm. He'd turned out to be more romantic than she could have ever imagined her good friend to be. Wonderfully, they were still the best of friends. When the roses he'd bought for her all wilted within a day, or when Wren threw a tantrum about not being able to go swimming with her friends, they could laugh and deal with it together.

Today, though, Wren's grandparents—all of them—would be at the event.

Just get through it.

Things with Blake's parents had been going pretty well. They'd been guarded at first, but Blake had talked to them, and Zoey had invited them over for a meal at her place, and they'd come to the diner for the first time ever. They'd gotten to know her, and she them, and they were all beginning to respect and like each other.

Carol Ann's parents were another story, or at least, they might be. They'd left for an extended cruise before Blake and Zoey's relationship had changed on Memorial Day, and they'd only arrived home a couple of days ago. This was the first time they'd see her and Blake together.

Would it be painful for them, seeing someone who wasn't Carol Ann on Blake's arm?

Zoey said a quick prayer as she, Blake and Wren joined the crowd mingling around the barbeque grills and picnic tables. Carol Ann's parents were nowhere in sight. Zoey didn't like the cowardice in her that hoped they wouldn't come.

She watched Blake talk with the pastor, then Geoff, then another dad whom she happened to know was a nuclear engineer. With everyone, he was respectful, interested and kind. She loved that about him.

She also loved his muscular strength as he helped move a couple of picnic tables around.

"There's Grammy and Grandpa!" Wren said, and they headed in the direction of Blake's parents.

They greeted each other, and then Mrs. Evans beckoned to her. "Can you help me get the Uber app on my phone?" she asked. "I don't want to ask Blake. He'll give me a lecture on how I have too many apps."

Zoey laughed. "He does tend to lecture," she said as they sat on a picnic bench. Zoey helped Mrs. Evans download the app and showed her how to use it. "You do have a lot of apps," she said. "I can help you organize them into folders, if you'd like."

"That would be wonderful, dear, but another time. I don't want to take you away from the fun." She patted Zoey's arm. "You're good with technology, you know, and you're good with people, too. You could go to school for it, if you wanted to."

Zoey shrugged. "Seems kind of late for that, and I do like my job." But she tucked the idea away to think about later.

The crowd was growing. Zoey rejoined Blake, and they greeted Cam and Jodi and their kids, then Alec and Kelly. Zinnia and Wren agreed to stay in sight of a parent at all times and then ran toward the playground at the edge of the park.

Fiscus got out of a car and walked toward the crowd. Almost as one, Cam and Alec headed toward their brother.

"They're worried about whether he's been drinking," Jodi explained.

"Alec says he's been steady at AA," Kelly added. "But a couple of his old friends came to town, and that can be a disaster for a recovering alcoholic."

The three brothers talked and were soon laughing. Apparently, disaster had been averted for the moment.

Zoey spotted Larry, the cook, chatting with another waitress. Rena, her boss, appeared to be arguing with Geoff, who was starting to become a good friend to Blake…once Blake had ascertained the man had been helping Zoey out of kindness and wasn't interested in her in a romantic way.

"Hey." Olivia came over to join Zoey just as Kelly and Jodi started walking toward their husbands. "How's it going?"

"It's good. Did they find another tenant for the empty apartment? I feel bad that I didn't move in after expressing interest in the place."

"Some weird guy moved in." Olivia rolled her eyes.

"I'd much rather have had you as a neighbor. But I'm glad we became closer friends." She and Olivia had started walking several mornings a week.

Zoey helped with setting out food and then joined Blake and Wren, who were in line to fill their plates. Then she wished she hadn't, because Carol Ann's parents had just joined the food line.

Wren gave them a one-armed hug—her injured arm was still wrapped and in a sling, mostly to remind her to be careful while it finished healing. Then she darted off to greet a friend. Someone called Blake to help with a grill that was flaming up too high.

That left Zoey alone with Carol Ann's parents. Karen wasted no time. "Blake tells me the two of you are dating," she said.

"We are." Zoey gathered her courage. "I know it's probably hard for you to see someone else with—"

Karen touched her arm, interrupting. "We've had quite a change of perspective since the car accident," she said. "Carol Ann is with the Lord and can't be hurt now. Wren needs you and so does Blake. I'm sorry for my attitude before." She paused. "I just wanted to let you know that I feel differently now. I welcome you into my family, and…" Her mouth worked a little. "I hope you'll continue accepting us into yours."

"Of course!" Zoey hugged the woman. Blake hurried over, obviously ready to run interference, but they involved him in a conversation about Wren. He raised his eyebrows at Zoey, and she nodded to him and squeezed his hand. Things were going to work out okay. Wren needed all of her grandparents, and she would have them without conflict, or without much.

As the fireworks started later that night, Blake suggested they put their blanket near the river's edge. Wren was fading, and after a few *oohs* and *ahhs*, she dozed off.

Blake tucked his jacket over her and then knelt beside Zoey. He reached into his pocket, and only then did Zoey realize the significance of his posture.

He was *kneeling* beside her. Did that mean…?

"Zoey," he said in a low voice, not waking Wren. "These last couple of months have been great. I've fallen even more in love with you. You're so smart and so much fun, and…well, I want to be with you for the rest of my life."

Tears rushed to her eyes, and her throat closed.

"Will you marry me?" he asked, holding up a box with a simple, beautiful diamond ring in it.

She felt tongue-tied.

Blake's face fell. "You can tell me the truth."

Love washed over her, and suddenly she could speak. *Wanted* to speak, to tell this man what he meant to her. "I want to be with you forever, too. You're the man of my dreams. You're smart, and kind, and funny. And you're *good*. I want to grow old with you. So yes, I would be honored to marry you."

His smile got impossibly broad. He kissed her, lightly, and slid the ring onto her finger. In the background, fireworks lit the sky.

They sat back and watched, arms around each other, and Zoey had never been happier.

After a particularly loud boom, Wren woke up and climbed into Zoey's lap.

"Can we tell her?" Zoey whispered to Blake.

He nodded. "Go ahead."

She leaned to whisper in Wren's ear. "Would it be okay with you if Daddy and I got married?"

Wren sat bolt upright, her sleepy eyes flying open. "You'd be my mommy for real and always?"

Zoey nodded. "We'd never forget your first mommy, but I would be your mommy from now on."

Wren tackled her with a hug.

"Easy!" Blake said, trying to disentangle them and then ending up a part of their hug instead.

As they all laughed together, Zoey looked at the stars and breathed out a prayer of thanks.

* * * * *

Check out Lee's other stories set in Holiday Point:

A Companion for Christmas

A free online read, Nanny for the Summer, *is available at Harlequin.com. And more to come!*

Dear Reader,

Thank you for reading *A Mother for His Child.* I loved writing this story of Mother's Day sadness that turns to joy, because like many women, I've had a few difficult Mother's Days. When I was trying to become a mother, it hurt to watch other women enjoying their babies and getting hugs and cards from their kids. Then I became an adoptive mom and realized that God had a perfect plan all along. My daughter, Grace, is the delight of my life, and I'm so glad I was forced to wait for His perfect timing.

If Mother's Day is difficult for you, please know I'm sending you hugs, along with a prayer that God will turn your troubles into joy.

Happy Mother's Day,
Lee

THE MOMMY LIST

Kathryn Springer

To Lindsey and Norah
I'm so blessed to call you my daughters. Even if we weren't related, I would still choose you as friends!

It is of the Lord's mercies that we are not consumed,
because his compassions fail not.
They are new every morning: great is thy faithfulness.
—*Lamentations* 3:22–23

Chapter One

"Hurry up, Daddy! I don't want to be late!"

"I'm right behind you." Gage Lawrence grabbed his jacket and followed his daughter out the door. He didn't have the heart to tell Ava that thanks to a last-minute phone call from one of his more demanding clients, they already were.

He hopped into the cab of his pickup and glanced at the clock on the dashboard. Tried not to wince. At least their destination was only a mile down the road.

Gage waited until he heard the click of Ava's seat belt before he put the truck into gear. "How was school?"

"I told everyone we're getting a puppy!" She practically sang the last word. "Savannah didn't believe me, though."

Yeah, well, Gage couldn't believe it, either. Ava had been begging for one for several years and Gage's answer was always the same. *When you're a little older.*

And that, in Dad-Speak, meant "when you have an apartment of your own." But here he was, totally caving. Not that Gage had a choice. Desperate measures and all that.

Even though the word "desperate" might be a bit of an exaggeration—or not—he was confident that his six-year-old daughter was responsible for her age and would take good care of a pet. And even though having a puppy in the house would add to the over-all craziness of life, it would keep Ava's mind off of other things.

Like finding a mom.

Over the past few weeks, his precocious daughter had started dropping a few not-so-subtle hints that she wouldn't mind having one of those, either, but Gage had refused to take the bait. Ava didn't seem to real-ize that for her to have a mom, Gage would have to find a woman he wanted to marry.

Been there, done that, had the broken heart to prove it. His daughter was the only good thing that had come out of Gage's failed relationship with Taylor Bishop and they were doing just fine on their own.

At least he'd thought so until he'd found Ava's list.

Most of the time, Gage discarded the bits of flot-sam and jetsam he found in Ava's jeans while check-ing pockets on laundry day, but the heart-shaped piece of notebook paper looked like something she might want to keep.

And it was a good thing he'd looked at it more closely.

Gage was certain the floor had shifted underneath his feet when he'd seen the words written in neat block letters at the top of the page.

TOP SECRET: MOMS

Underneath the title was a list of names. A few of them misspelled, but proof that not only had his daughter *not* given up on finding a mom, she'd gone

one step further and created a list of potential candidates.

Well, Ava's secret was out.

Leaving Gage with no choice but to come up with a mission of his own. Dodge, deflect, distract.

"Are we there yet?" Ava pressed her freckled nose against the window and Gage chuckled.

"I haven't heard you ask that question since you were three."

"But this time we're picking out a puppy!" Ava grinned. And no matter how exhausted Gage was after a ten-hour workday, those grins fell like a sunbeam on his soul, melting away any leftover tension caused by deadlines or disgruntled clients or canceled deliveries.

"There might not be a puppy," Gage warned. "Sometimes dogs that are surrendered or abandoned are older. We'll have to see when we get there."

Gage didn't have a preference as to the breed or age. His main concern was that it be housebroken. And quiet. Quiet would be good.

As they rounded a corner, he spotted a battered mailbox on the side of the road and slowed down.

If it hadn't been for Connie, his office manager, Gage wouldn't have known the old McMurphy place on the edge of town had recently changed hands. There'd been no For Sale sign at the end of the driveway. No ad in the newspaper. No phone call from a Realtor, or a member of the previous owner's family, wondering if Gage would be interested in purchasing the property adjacent to his—which he might have been, given the opportunity.

Neil McMurphy had passed away over a decade ago but his siblings had continued to meet at the property once a summer for their family reunion. A few years ago, Gage had heard a rumor that travel had become a challenge for some of the older relatives so they'd closed up the house for good and opted for a more central gathering place instead.

He could only imagine what kind of shape it was in after being vacant for so long, but the scattering of small outbuildings would have appealed to a buyer seeking a spacious piece of property for a dog rescue.

Connie had somehow become privy to that information, too.

Gage considered it almost providential that he'd found out about the new owner's plans the day after he'd stumbled upon Ava's list. When he'd asked a few more questions, his extremely efficient office manager had earned another bonus by giving him said owner's name—Megan Albright—along with a phone number.

Gage turned onto the narrow gravel road across from the mailbox. It wound through a stand of mixed hardwoods and pine that served as a natural buffer between the McMurphy place and Gage's property.

Ava could hardly contain her excitement as the house came into view.

Shadows had already started to fill the pockets between the trees and Gage glanced at the clock on the dashboard again.

Thirty minutes late.

But someone who took in dogs that no one else

wanted would be the type of person who believed in extending a little grace, right?

A dog barreled around the corner of the house and Ava squealed.

"Look, Daddy! Do you think that one needs a home?"

Gage certainly hoped not.

The animal, with its shaggy black coat and massive head, looked more like a bear fresh out of hibernation than a dog. It made a beeline straight for his truck. Fortunately, it braked at the same time Gage did and began to bark rather than take a bite out of the tires.

But then Gage made the colossal mistake of rolling his window down. Colossal because he hadn't realized the dog would take the gesture as an invitation to jump up and plant his muddy paws on the ledge of the opening, bringing them nose to nose.

The swipe of a wet tongue across Gage's jaw coincided with a piercing whistle. The dog managed to get one more lick in before dropping to all fours and ambling back to the woman who'd summoned him.

The brim of a faded ball cap shadowed her face, obscuring her features. She walked toward them, a slight hitch in each measured step, and stopped a few yards from the truck. Caught Gage in the act of wiping away the residue from the dog's exuberant greeting.

"Mr. Lawrence?" Her voice was pitched low, soft but melodic, like the creek that ran through the back of Gage's property.

At Gage's nod, she reached down to give one of the behemoth's furry ears a scratch. "Sorry about that.

We're still working on manners. I only let Baxter out-side because I didn't think you'd be coming over this evening after all."

When she lifted her head again, Gage felt a jolt of surprise. Wisps of sun-streaked brown hair had es-caped from the ponytail threaded through the back of her cap, framing a face with sculpted cheekbones, a short, straight nose, and eyes the deep violet-blue of a summer sky.

Two thoughts registered in Gage's head at exactly the same time.

Megan Albright—their new neighbor and cham-pion of dogs in need of rescue—couldn't have been over thirty.

And she was pretty. Really pretty.

Gage glanced in the rearview mirror, saw Ava's re-flection, and stifled a groan.

Because his daughter was grinning again.

For some reason, Megan had pictured Gage Law-rence as a middle-aged businessman with kind eyes and a benevolent smile.

She'd only moved to Pine Bridge a few weeks ago, but during an enlightening conversation with Ron, who worked at the local hardware store, she'd discov-ered that Triple L Builders employed a quarter of the people who lived in the area.

She'd also found out that Gage Lawrence, the owner of said company, donated generously to projects that benefited the community. When Gage had left a mes-sage on Megan's cell asking if he could meet with her, she'd hoped the local grapevine had worked in her favor and that he'd wanted to learn more about the rescue.

This Gage Lawrence was close to her age. And his eyes, more suspicious than kind, remained locked on Baxter.

No benevolent smile, either.

But it wasn't her fault the Newfoundland mix, who tended to forget about boundaries when it came to public displays of affection, had been the first one to greet him.

Five minutes after their scheduled appointment time, she'd assumed Gage Lawrence was running a little late. At the fifteen-minute mark, Megan had checked her phone for messages.

Nothing. No text. No voice mail. No apology for getting her hopes up.

Gage Lawrence had either forgotten about their appointment—the one that *he'd* made—or something more important had come up.

Megan had let Baxter outside and just slid a pizza in the oven when she'd heard Bax's someone-is-here-to-play-with-me bark.

Except that Gage Lawrence didn't look like he wanted to play. In fact, it looked like he was debating whether or not to get out of the truck.

The door to the back seat suddenly flew open. The windows of the pickup were tinted, so Megan hadn't realized Gage wasn't alone, but the little girl who vaulted to the ground didn't seem to share his reservations. The bright smile on her face reminded Megan of a kid on Christmas morning.

"Hi! I'm Ava!" she announced.

Even with a crown of blonde curls and a scattering of butterscotch freckles sprinkled across her nose, Megan instantly noted the resemblance between the two in the curve of their jaw and hazel eyes.

"Hello, Ava. I'm Megan." She put her hand on Baxter's head, gently reminding him of guest protocol as the bushy tail began to thump out a welcome beat against the ground. "And this is Baxter."

"Hold on, sweetheart."

Megan's gaze slid to the man who'd finally hopped down from the cab of the pickup. Long, jeans-clad legs ate up the distance between them. He placed himself between his daughter and Baxter like a protective six-foot wall.

Megan tamped down a sigh.

Caution was always wise when meeting a dog for the first time, of course, but Gage's reaction told Megan that he belonged with the category of people who equated "rescue" with "risky."

When Megan had been laying the groundwork for Homeward Bound, she'd heard stories about people who assumed dog rescues housed dirty, dangerous animals that barked constantly and lowered the property value of the neighborhood. Education was part of Megan's vision, as important as donations when it came to starting a rescue, and she looked forward to changing people's perceptions. Although some of them—like the man standing in her driveway—might require a little more time.

"But he's wagging his tail, Dad." Ava peeked around the immovable obstacle of denim and flannel that was her father, willing, it seemed, to give Baxter the benefit of the doubt.

Megan gave Baxter's head another pat and motioned to Ava to join her. "Baxter is very friendly but sometimes he forgets how big he is."

Ava peeked up at Gage through a fringe of golden lashes, her eyes beseeching as she waited for permission to pet the dog. When he nodded, Ava scurried over to Megan's side.

For once, Bax didn't take advantage of the situation and introduce himself to their guest with a sloppy kiss to the cheek. He did, however, lift one of his dinner-plate-size paws for her to shake.

"He's so cute!" Ava complied with a giggle. "If you don't have any puppies, can we adopt him?"

Megan blinked.

Adopt him?

"Baxter isn't—" Megan's watch began to beep and she tapped the screen. "I'm sorry. My pizza is ready to come out of the oven."

She hadn't meant it as a subtle reprimand, a reminder that Gage had turned their late-afternoon appointment into a dinner meeting, but his brows dipped together.

"I'm the one who should be apologizing." Gage's rich-as-dark-chocolate voice flowed over her. "A phone call came in right when I was leaving work—"

"Dad gets a lot of phone calls," Ava interjected with a sigh.

Gage's frown deepened but he didn't deny it.

"I had to stop by the house to change clothes first," he continued. "But I should have called to let you know we were on our way."

Yes, he should have. He should have mentioned he was bringing his daughter, too. And that he was interested in adopting a dog.

Megan rubbed the ache that bloomed in her thigh and glanced at Ava. The sudden droop in the girl's slim shoulders told Megan she'd figured out the alarm meant they'd have to come back another time.

"You're welcome to come inside," Megan heard herself say. "We can chat a bit while the pizza cools."

Chapter Two

Megan looked as surprised by the unexpected offer as Gage was.

But he'd set aside time for the appointment and who knew when another slot would open up in his week if he turned down the invitation?

"If you're sure you don't mind," Gage said.

Megan didn't look sure, but Ava was already skipping toward the house.

The builder in Gage took over as they walked up the drive.

Neil McMurphy had been a bit of a recluse but even though the house was structurally sound—Gage knew this because his dad had built the log home over twenty years ago—it would benefit from some cosmetic updates. Scaly patches of moss clung to the shingles and the extreme temperature changes, a fact of life in Wisconsin, had scoured away the finish on the logs.

He scanned the outbuildings, looking for something that confirmed Megan Albright had opened a dog rescue. But there were no kennels. Not even a sign with the name and logo.

The only proof that Connie had been right about Megan's plans was the voice mail she'd left on Gage's phone, confirming their appointment, and the hundred-pound mop that had attached itself to his daughter's side.

Gage shifted his attention back to Megan.

She'd slowed down, her brow furrowed in concentration as she carefully navigated the uneven path of paving stones that connected the driveway to the house.

Gage hadn't imagined the slight hitch in her step. Hadn't missed the way she'd absently rubbed her hip in much the same way she'd rubbed the dog's ear, like she was reminding it to behave.

Gage wanted to offer his arm for support but the tilt in Megan's chin said she was doing just fine, thank you. And when it came to his new neighbor, Gage had probably reached his quota of mistakes for the day.

Megan climbed the steps to the porch and the scent of warm bread and garlic washed over them when she opened the door.

Gage's stomach growled in appreciation. He hadn't eaten since…

He couldn't remember; a clue that it had been a while. He'd washed a stale donut down with a cup of coffee on his way to a building site midmorning, but wasn't sure that qualified as a meal.

Baxter shuffled over to a dog bed not much smaller than Ava's twin mattress. He picked up a braided rope and shook it, a signal that he wanted to play. Ava grabbed the other end and started a lively game of tug-of-war.

"Excuse me." Megan went straight to the kitchen

to remove the pizza from the oven, giving Gage an opportunity to check out the interior.

He'd only been inside the house once, when Neil had asked for help replacing a broken pipe, but Gage remembered oversize, tobacco-brown leather furniture that had taken up every square inch of the living room. In lieu of paintings or photographs, Neil had created a bragging wall with the largemouth bass he'd caught over the years.

Like the furniture, the fish had disappeared. Megan hadn't lived there very long but she'd added a more feminine touch to the rustic décor. Facing the stone fireplace was a small but comfortable-looking sofa and two chairs, all of them covered in a durable fabric the same shade of green as the buds on the trees. Without the heavy drapes that had once given the room a cavelike feel, the last of the evening sunlight streamed through the windows and dappled the hardwood floor.

Ava pulled in a breath, startling him. "Daddy, look! There's another dog!"

Gage traced the invisible line between Ava's pointing finger and the kitchen, where a full-grown Dalmatian pressed against Megan's side, eyeing them suspiciously.

Ava took a step forward, ready to make another friend, but Megan shook her head.

"This is Tux, and he's a little shy around strangers," she said. "Let's let him decide when he's ready to say hello, all right?"

Ava nodded vigorously. "My best friend Willow

is shy, too," she said. "She doesn't like it when Miss Peake calls on her during story time."

If Gage remembered correctly, Ava's Sunday school teacher had been her first choice for a mom. Hannah Peake was single, pretty and barely out of high school, too. Age hadn't seemed to be a determining factor, though, because Eliza Owens, their silver-haired mail carrier, had also made his daughter's list.

A smile tugged at the corner of Megan's lips and Gage felt a corresponding tug on his heart. "I'm glad you understand how Tux feels."

"What kind of pizza is that?" Ava paused the game of tug-of-war and dashed into the kitchen, rising up on her tiptoes at the counter for a better look. "It smells soooo good!"

"I call it the kitchen sink," Megan said. "Whatever is in the fridge goes on top. Tonight, it's spinach, onions and mushrooms. And cheese, of course."

"You made it all by yourself?" Ava's eyes went wide. "Dad's too busy to cook very much. When we want pizza, he picks it up at Franco's."

Not always, Gage wanted to protest. Sometimes they came from the freezer aisle at the grocery store.

Megan opened one of the cupboards and retrieved not one but three plates. "There's plenty." She winked at Ava. "If you don't mind the spinach."

"Miss Albright…" Gage choked out. This time, he had no problem coming to their neighbor's rescue. "Ava and I are not going to eat your dinner."

But while Gage was silently reminding his daughter that this was an appointment, not a social call, Ava was already reaching for a plate.

Megan couldn't remember the last time she'd had company for dinner.

Weeks. Months.

Eight, to be exact.

Before she'd fallen through the floor of a burning house and ended up on the concrete surface of the basement.

During her recovery, Megan had been the recipient of a lot of meals, but this was the first time she'd been the one to prepare and serve one to someone else.

And it felt...kind of good, actually.

That was why Megan decided to ignore the parental warning Gage was attempting to send his daughter through a series of head shakes and meaningful looks, and nudged a plate toward him.

"Thank you," Gage muttered. "Again."

Megan smiled. A smart man knew when he was outnumbered.

"I haven't bought a dining room table and chairs yet, but there's some old patio furniture on the screen porch," she told him. "It's nice enough this evening, so we can sit out there."

"What can I do to help?" Gage stepped around the half wall that separated the living room from the kitchen and the space seemed to shrink to half its size.

Tux noticed, too, and pressed his head against Megan's knee, triggering a fire that spread all the way down to her toes.

"Nothing." She practically gasped the word.

The orthopedic surgeon had warned Megan that ligaments and tendons were the slowest parts of the body to heal. Megan's accident had shredded both and there were times when her knee reminded her of that.

But at least she hadn't toppled over this time.

Progress.

Megan was thankful for every little sign.

"We already crashed your dinner," Gage pointed out, a glint of humor in his eyes. "Do you want me to feel useless *and* guilty?"

"Fine. There's a pitcher of water in the fridge," Megan said. "Glasses in the cupboard on the left."

While Gage was taking care of the beverages, she lured Tux out of the kitchen and into his crate with a biscuit. He was a sweetheart but nervous around people he didn't know, especially men. Healing required patience.

A lesson Megan had been learning since the accident.

"Do you have a tray?" Gage asked.

"Um...somewhere?" Megan admitted. Half the contents of her former apartment was still in boxes in the extra bedroom, waiting to be unpacked. The sale had moved quickly and Megan had only "toured" the home online. She knew she'd bought a house that needed a little TLC, but if Megan didn't count the mice, no one had lived on the premises for over three years. Since she'd moved in, the majority of her time and energy had been spent cleaning and turning the house into a home again.

"No problem. We'll improvise," Gage said.

To her astonishment, he ran his fingers along the edge of the butcher-block counter, paused for a moment and then, right before Megan's eyes, a cutting board slid out.

"How did you know that was there?"

Gage smiled. "It's standard issue in every Log Living by Lawrence kitchen."

"We have one, too," Ava chimed in.

Because Gage's smile was more distracting than discovering there were secret hiding places in Megan's new house, it took a moment to process what he'd said.

Log Living by Lawrence.

Now Megan knew how Triple L Builders had gotten its name.

"Did you build the house down the road, too? The one with the stone chimney?" Megan caught a glimpse of the massive two-story log home through the trees every time she drove into town. It was almost the end of April now, but once the leaves came out, the foliage would form a natural hedge between their properties.

Ava giggled. "That's ours!"

Megan stared at her. "*Yours?*"

"My dad remarried a few years ago and he and his wife decided they wanted to travel more," Gage explained. "I grew up there, but Dad sold it to me so they could buy an RV."

Megan had hoped that whoever lived on the adjoining property liked dogs, but for some reason the thought of Gage being her closest neighbor rattled her a bit.

Maybe because he didn't miss anything.

Like her limp.

She got the feeling that Gage Lawrence was in a constant state of motion, but she'd noticed that he'd slowed down, matched his pace to hers, when they'd walked up the driveway. He'd also stuck close on the path-turned-obstacle course, almost as if he were anticipating she'd stumble in one of the cracks and fall flat on her face.

"Anything else? I can grab the pizza, too."

Megan battled a sudden wave of discouragement. As a firefighter, she'd carried over half her body weight in equipment every time she'd gone on a call. Even with two pins in her wrist, she could carry a pizza from one room to another. It was the trick knee that Megan didn't completely trust.

"Sure."

Like patience, accepting help was something she'd been working on, too.

Gage set the glasses on the cutting board and balanced the pizza pan in the crook of his arm like the seasoned waitstaff at a fancy restaurant.

"Ava? Door, please."

She bounced across the kitchen and held it open while Gage and Megan filed through. They all claimed a seat around the wicker table and Megan divided up the pizza.

"We have to say grace, Daddy!" Ava laced her fingers together and bowed her head. "Thank You, God, for this food. And for a wonderful day. And thank You for puppies."

Ava's prayer would have provided the perfect segue for finding out more about the Lawrence family but it was Gage who asked the first question.

"So, what brought you to Pine Bridge?" He handed Ava a napkin. "Do you have family in the area?"

Megan shook her head. "I'm from Eau Claire. My parents moved to Arizona after I graduated, but my grandma still lives there. A friend of mine heard I was looking for a house with a little bit of property and mentioned that her aunts and uncles were considering selling a place they'd inherited from a family member.

"She emailed me some photos with the caveat that they didn't want to put any money into renovations before it went on the market. A few touchups didn't scare me, and they accepted my offer."

An offer only made possible because of her grandma Lou's generosity. She'd insisted that investing in Megan's dreams was something she would never regret. Grandma Lou had encouraged Megan's dream of becoming a firefighter, too, but this one—starting over with a new home, a new career—seemed riskier. Stretched Megan's faith the same way the physical therapist had coaxed her to stretch her muscles even when it hurt.

"Did you operate a dog rescue there, too?" Gage asked.

A knot formed in Megan's throat as the innocent question pressed on another wound that hadn't quite healed yet.

Chapter Three

Say. Something.

"No." Acutely aware that Gage was waiting for an answer, Megan managed to push out the word.

Talking about the job she'd loved was as painful as the injuries she'd sustained. The reconstructive surgery on her knee had been deemed a success, but the doctors hadn't been able to save her career. She could wield a paintbrush but not a fire hose. Climb stairs but not a ladder in her turnout gear. "But Baxter and Tux were my inspiration."

"Did you adopt them?" Ava wanted to know.

"I did." A smile surfaced at the bittersweet memory. In a way, the two dogs had rescued *her*.

"Oh." Ava looked disappointed for a moment but then her smile surfaced again. "I want a puppy but I don't mind a growed-up dog like Baxter. Daddy said we had to wait to see if it's a boy or a girl before I can pick out a collar, though."

Megan cast a glance at Gage, who was polishing off the last piece of pizza on his plate.

Was he under the impression they would be taking a dog home with them today? Matching a dog with the right family was a process that shouldn't be rushed, but Megan didn't want to dim the sparkle in the little girl's eyes.

"That's a good idea," she said. "How about you

keep Baxter company for a few minutes while I talk to your daddy?"

Ava bobbed her head. "Okay!"

Gage reached for the empty pizza pan but Megan stopped him.

"Don't worry about cleaning up. We can go into my office and pull up your application."

Megan's "office" was a glorified storage closet at the back of the house; it would have to suffice for now. She hadn't expected a response so quickly after her website had gone live but, thanks to Gage, she knew it was working.

At least Megan *thought* the links were working. The confused expression on Gage's face left room for doubt.

"Application?" he repeated.

"Ava mentioned a puppy, so I assume that's why you're here? The application is one of the requirements for adoption. The link was posted on the website, along with my phone number."

Gage still looked confused. And then he cleared his throat. "Right. I guess I missed that part. I'll fill it out right now."

"Mr. Lawrence—" Megan began.

"Gage."

"Gage," she amended. "There's no need to rush it. I'm sure you've figured out that I don't have any dogs available for adoption at the moment."

The man owned a building company. He had to have noticed the fencing stacked by the pole shed, waiting to be turned into outdoor runs for the kennels as soon as Megan found someone to do the work. The lumber, which she'd covered with a tarp, would eventually line the walls of the indoor exercise area.

Once again, the enormity of the task threatened to overwhelm Megan.

A step at a time, Grandma Lou would say. Words of wisdom Megan had heard from her therapist, too. But for some reason, she didn't think Gage Lawrence adhered to that particular code. He seemed more like a pedal-to-the-metal-let's-get-this-done kind of guy.

"But filling out an application will start the process, right? Put us on the list?"

"Yes…" Megan drew out the word.

"Then I'd just as soon take care of it now," Gage said, proving Megan's theory. "If you don't mind."

"All right." She pulled up the file on her laptop and printed out a copy.

Gage managed to squeeze his muscular frame into a metal folding chair, pen and application in hand. A swatch of sable hair dipped over Gage's forehead as he bent his head. There was something charming in his low huff of frustration as he swept it back into place, as if it were a frequent battle, and Megan realized she was smiling.

She was also staring.

"Um… I'll be right back."

Ava and Baxter, sprawled out on the rug, were playing tug-of-war with Baxter's rope when Megan checked on them.

Gage's daughter grinned up at her. "He's winning!"

Ava Lawrence was charming, too. And responsible,

judging from the way she'd carried her empty plate to the kitchen after dinner without being prompted.

"Baxter loves tug-of-war as much as he loves a good tummy rub," Megan told her.

Ava's gaze shifted to Tux, who was watching them intently from behind the door of his crate. "Do you like tug-of-war?" she asked, her voice whisper-soft. "I'll play with you, too."

Tux whined deep in his throat but the thump of his stubby tail told Megan that he was warming up to their guests.

She unlatched the door and Tux instantly attached himself to Megan's side.

"Would you like to give them a treat?" she asked Ava.

The girl nodded eagerly and followed her into the kitchen. Megan took two biscuits from a ceramic canister on the counter and handed them to Ava.

"Be gentlemen," she reminded the dogs.

Ava giggled when they politely took the biscuits from her hand. Both disappeared in a single bite.

"I hope we get a dog as nice as Baxter and Tux," she said, her voice wistful.

"Have you ever had one before?" Megan asked.

"Daddy said we had to wait 'til I was bigger, but he changed his mind."

Megan made a mental note to find out why.

She left Ava and Baxter playing a second round of their game while Tux accompanied her back to the office.

Gage looked up.

"This application is five pages long." He handed it back to her. "A detailed description of my house and yard. Questions about my interests and hobbies. References. I don't think the bank asked for this much information the last time I took out a business loan."

Megan couldn't tell if Gage was teasing or not as she skimmed through the application.

On the last set of questions that pertained specifically to his current lifestyle, Gage had written that his forty-hour-plus workweek often included evenings and weekends. He hadn't listed any hobbies, either.

Or anyone else living in their household, which meant there wasn't a Mrs. Lawrence...

Megan pushed that thought aside. Gage Lawrence's marital status wasn't any of her business except for the fact that the bulk of the day-to-day responsibilities would fall to him and Ava.

"You work a lot of hours," she said.

"It comes with the territory." Gage's broad shoulders lifted and fell in a shrug. "I used to be Dad's second-in-command but after I took over the company, I haven't replaced myself yet."

"There are a lot of dogs with pedigrees available." Megan's gaze shifted to Gage again. "Why did you decide on a rescue?"

"Why not?" Gage countered. "They need homes, too."

"True," Megan said carefully. "But a pet is a long-term commitment and sometimes the dogs that come in require medical care. Socialization. Preparing them for another change can be a lengthy process until they're ready to be placed with a family."

Something flickered in Gage's eyes. "How lengthy?"

"I won't be able to answer that until I have a chance to evaluate them." Megan tipped her head, considering not the question itself but the motivation behind it. "Is Ava's birthday coming up? Is that why you're anxious to adopt?"

To her astonishment, a hint of red bloomed underneath the grain of stubble on Gage's angular jaw.

"Her birthday? No."

Megan was relieved to hear it. Too many people adopted pets as birthday or Christmas gifts, only to realize that after the initial excitement died down, there was a living, breathing animal in the home. One that required food, exercise, grooming and a lot more attention than a stuffed toy the child could set on a shelf at the end of the day.

"Companionship, then?" Megan guessed. "Protection?"

To her astonishment, the color deepened.

"A little bit of both," Gage muttered.

Companionship for Ava, protection for him, but he couldn't tell Megan that without mentioning The List.

He watched her flip the page over and relaxed a little when she skimmed the section pertaining to his hobbies and interests.

"You're on the city council," Megan murmured. "An active member of the Pine Bridge parks and rec-

reation committee. You oversee the volunteer main-
tenance crew at your church."

"They needed someone to fill those positions after
my dad left."

It had taken a while, but Gage had finally earned his
place in the community. Earned the respect of both his
father and the people who'd doubted that Gage would
succeed at anything, especially after he'd quit college his senior year and returned to Pine Bridge with
a newborn baby instead of a degree in architecture.

"Member of the Half-Pint Pitchers Club?" Megan
looked up, a question in her eyes.

"Baseball." Gage smiled. "Some of the younger kids
were feeling left out because they couldn't play. I lined
up a few coaches to work on some basic skills."

Megan dipped her chin in a nod and flipped to the
last page, which included the names and phone numbers of half a dozen people who would attest to the
fact that not only was Gage a model citizen, he would
be a model pet owner, too.

So why was Megan nibbling on her lower lip? Staring at his application as if he'd put Cruella de Vil down
as a reference?

He owned a house in the country, with plenty of
room for a dog to stretch its legs. Ran a successful
company. Volunteered in the community.

"Is there a problem?" Gage believed in tackling
them head-on. "Do you think Ava is too young for a
pet? Because she's very responsible. She's been asking for a dog since she could say the word, and I know
she will take good care of it."

"I don't doubt that for a moment," Megan said. "But based on what you wrote…well…you have a very busy life."

Gage blinked as her words sank in.

"Wait a second. You're saying *I'm* the weak link here?"

Megan's lips twitched. "I'm saying you don't seem to be home very often."

Gage couldn't deny it. But…

"A lot of working people have pets," he pointed out. "Isn't the goal to place dogs with a family of their own?"

"But it has to be a good fit for the dog *and* the family or the dog will end up without a home again." Megan's eyes clouded. "That's what happened to Tux. Twice."

Gage understood now why Megan's screening process was so rigorous, but still. It was the first time he felt like a failure for being…successful.

It probably hadn't helped Gage's case that he'd been late for their appointment due to a work-related phone call, either.

"I'll look this over more thoroughly when I have time," Megan murmured.

Gage wanted to press the issue, but the shadows on the wall reminded him that it was a school night for Ava.

"I appreciate it…and dinner, too."

"You're welcome." Megan smiled now. "I'm glad you and Ava stayed. As sweet as the pups are, they don't contribute much in the way of dinner conversation."

The comment made Gage more curious about his

new neighbor, but she set the application on her desk, a hint the interview portion of the meeting was over.

"Ava! Time to go home." Gage strode into the living room and spotted his daughter sitting on the floor. Baxter was sprawled beside her, his furry chin resting on her knee.

"He likes me, Daddy! Can I come back tomorrow and play with him?" Ava's hopeful gaze bounced from Gage to Megan and back again.

"I have to work late tomorrow, sweetheart," Gage said.

Out of the corner of his eye, he saw Megan's frown and realized he'd unintentionally confirmed her suspicions that a dog might not fit seamlessly into the Lawrence family's lifestyle.

"Okay." Ava patted Baxter's head as she hopped to her feet.

And then, before Gage could stop her, his affectionate, extroverted daughter skipped over to Megan and gave her a quick hug.

"Thanks for the pizza! And for letting me play with Baxter!"

"You're welcome," Megan said, her voice husky.

"We'll come back soon and maybe you'll have our dog!"

Megan didn't answer as she saw them to the door, leaving Gage to draw one conclusion.

Not only would the Lawrences *not* be getting another invitation to dinner anytime soon, they wouldn't be adopting a dog from the Homeward Bound Rescue, either.

Chapter Four

"You're late, Daddy."

Ava climbed into the back seat and waved at Mrs. Hayes, the only adult present on the now-empty playground.

"I'm sorry." As soon as Gage uttered the words, he realized he'd been saying them way too much this week.

Ordinarily, he picked Ava up at three o'clock when school ended for the day, drove her home, and returned phone calls while she changed her clothes and ate a snack. But putting out fires at various job sites had thrown his schedule off-kilter and Gage was having a hard time playing catch-up. Now it was after five and Mrs. Hayes hadn't looked happy as she disappeared inside the building.

"Are you buckled?"

"Not yet." Ava was unzipping her backpack. "Mrs. Hayes sent a note!"

Oh, boy.

He wasn't *that* late—ten...okay, fifteen—minutes, but there were strict rules about pickup for the after-school program and Gage had broken them. Twice.

He was already devising another apology in the form of a gift certificate from The Three Chocolatiers candy shop on Main Street when Ava thrust an envelope over the back of his seat.

"Open it, Daddy!" Ava could hardly contain her excitement while Gage eyed the innocent-looking white envelope with trepidation.

"Can it wait until we get home?"

So far today, in addition to his normal responsibilities, Gage had gotten a call from a frustrated member of his carpentry crew, who'd arrived at a job site only to find the road blocked by a truck delivering appliances to a house that didn't have walls let alone a kitchen. After that was a surveyor, asking Gage if he knew there was a dispute brewing between one of his clients and the neighbor who owned the property next door.

Now Samantha Hayes, his daughter's first-grade teacher, had sent him a handwritten note, no doubt reminding Gage that he needed to step up his game on the parental front, too.

"Uh-uh." In response to his question, Ava shook her head so hard the ponytail Gage had attempted to put in her hair that morning slapped against the window. "Please?"

A six-year-old's superpower. Turning a one-syllable word into three.

Gage buried a sigh and slid his thumbnail underneath the flap, breaking the seal. Ava was hanging over the seat now, watching him remove the contents of the envelope. He unfolded the piece of paper inside and relaxed a little. No official letterhead with a copy of the after-school pickup rules that Gage expected to find. This was all Ava, from the meticulous letters that spelled out her name to the outline of two small hands framed in cheerful bands of pink and yellow.

"I made it!" Ava said proudly. "Mrs. Hayes helped us trace our hands but she let us dec'rate it with the colors we like the best."

"I love it," Gage said. "And I think there's even room on the fridge—"

"It's not for you, Daddy." Ava giggled. "It's for Miss Megan."

Miss Megan.

And just like that, an image of the woman Gage had been trying *not* to think about the past few days popped into his mind.

"It's for our Hearts and Hands project," Ava chattered on. "We're s'posed to give it to someone who needs our help."

It wasn't that he was opposed to Ava volunteering a few hours at the rescue, but the reality was, Gage couldn't think of anything she was old enough to do. Megan's most pressing needs seemed to be getting the kennels and outdoor runs ready for any four-legged guests that would arrive.

He'd noticed the fencing stacked beside the shed. The pyramid of unopened paint cans in the corner of the screened porch where they'd eaten dinner. The tower of boxes in Megan's office that had yet to be unpacked.

What Megan had already accomplished was admirable, but the amount of work required to get the rescue up and running would keep their new neighbor busy twenty-four-seven.

"Can we drop it off at Miss Megan's house on our way home?" Ava was asking. "Mrs. Hayes said everyone has to pick a project by tomorrow."

"Like you said, it's getting late." Gage hedged. "It's more polite to call first than to show up at someone's door."

"Okay!" Ava's seat belt clicked into place. "Can you call her on the way home?"

Gage could see there was no getting out of this.

He'd put the rescue in his list of contacts, so he set the paper on the passenger seat and punched Megan's number on his cell. The Bluetooth picked it up as he pulled into the street.

One. Two. Three rings. Gage was about to end the call when Megan's voice came over the line.

"You've reached Megan Albright at Homeward Bound Rescue. I can't take your call right now but please leave a message and I'll get back to you as soon as I can. Thank you."

Gage hung up before the beep. "Megan must be busy right now, but I'll try again later."

"Okay." Ava sighed, her disappointment almost palpable.

Lately, the main topics of conversation at breakfast and dinner had revolved around two things: Megan and the rescue.

And Gage had no one to blame but himself.

"What else did you do in school today?" he asked, hoping to distract her.

"I finished my math sheet so Mrs. Hayes let me check out a book from the library."

"What's it about?" Gage cracked his window. The scent of last night's rain and the sound of spring peepers flowed into the cab of the truck.

"A dog named Pickles."

A dog.

Why wasn't Gage surprised?

"Pickles is smaller than Baxter, though," Ava told him.

Gage's zero-turn mower was smaller than Baxter.

He turned onto their road and heard Ava gasp. "There she is, Daddy! Miss Megan!"

Sure enough, Megan was walking down her driveway toward the house, Tux the Dalmatian at her side.

"Now you don't have to call her back and it'll still be polite if we stop 'cause we're not showing up at her door."

Gage couldn't argue with that logic. Especially when Megan had heard the vehicle approaching and paused to clip on the dog's leash.

Today she wore hiking boots and the baggy overalls again, layered over a T-shirt the same shade of blue as her eyes.

Ava unbuckled, retrieved the envelope and bailed out of the truck the moment Gage turned off the engine. She took a few bouncing steps toward Megan but promptly slowed down when Tux ducked his head and pressed against Megan's side.

Megan said something to the dog before she cast a warm smile in Ava's direction.

Gage realized there was no delaying the inevitable and swung down from the cab.

"I made something for you." Ava held up the envelope, barely able to contain her excitement. "You can open it now."

"All right." Megan looked a little bemused by Ava's enthusiasm but she opened the flap and removed the piece of paper with the tracing of Ava's hands. Her lips curved in a smile. "I happen to love pink and yellow. Thank you, Ava."

"We're supposed to pick someone to help for our Hearts and Hands project at school and I picked you!"

"Me?" Megan echoed. Her gaze shifted to Gage. "I'm not sure what a…a Hearts and Hands project involves."

"Mrs. Hayes wants everyone in the first-grade class to volunteer a few hours of their time to a worthy cause every week," Gage explained.

"Uh-huh." Ava bobbed her head. "I can do a lot of stuff to help. I can feed the dogs. Take Baxter for a walk. And Dad knows how to fix stuff."

Whoa.

Dad?

It suddenly occurred to Gage that his six-year-old daughter wasn't going to drive herself back and forth from home to the rescue.

"That's very sweet of you," Megan murmured.

Suddenly, Ava frowned. "What happened? Does that hurt?"

She was looking at Megan's arm, so Gage's gaze naturally moved in that direction, too. His breath caught in his throat.

A jagged scar extended from Megan's elbow to her

wrist and even though Gage wasn't a doctor, he could tell by the bright pink color that whatever had caused the injury hadn't happened all that long ago.

Gage opened his mouth to remind his daughter that her question fell under the category of "personal," but his eyes met Megan's and she almost imperceptibly shook her head.

"A little," she told Ava. "But it's getting better every day."

Gage couldn't help but notice she hadn't answered Ava's question about *how* the injury had come about.

Their new neighbor was a mystery, no doubt about it. The more Gage found out about Megan, the more questions he had.

One thing he did know for certain.

She could use some help.

Megan had been asking God for help.

But she'd thought the response would come in the form of a faster recovery than her physical therapist had predicted. A call from the carpenter, telling Megan the rescue had moved up a notch or two on his waiting list. What she hadn't considered was that an adorable first-grader would be the answer to her prayer.

The fact that first-grader had a father who just happened to own a construction company and would know which outbuildings were structurally sound and which ones should be demolished was the kind of thing Grandma Lou liked to call a "God-size surprise."

And the offer of help was certainly a surprise, considering Megan had expressed concern about Gage's application.

"You mentioned there were some things you had to finish before you could open the rescue," Gage said. "If you give us an idea what they are, we can come up with a plan and go from there."

Megan *had* mentioned that. And a few hours ago, another item had been added to her lengthy to-do list.

She'd been outside, slowly removing years of debris from Neil McMurphy's toolshed, when Jacqueline Price had called. Jac was the vet tech who'd introduced Megan to Baxter and now she had another challenge in the form of a ten-year-old yellow Lab.

"I don't know what else to do with CB, Meg. He's been here for three days and he refuses to eat. I'm worried he's depressed," Jac had told her. "I know the rescue isn't officially up and running yet, but could you take him for a few days? I'm hoping a change of scenery will help."

Megan couldn't say no. Just like she couldn't say no to Ava Lawrence, either.

She tucked the paper back inside the envelope and looked at Gage. Drew in a breath and released it again.

"All right. If this is a school assignment, what kind of timeline are we looking at?"

Gage's warm smile inexplicably sowed goose bumps up Megan's arms.

"We can go up to the house and you can show us some of the things that need to be done right now, if you'd like."

Ava clapped her hands. "Are we having pizza again?"

Gage winced and cast an apologetic look at Megan before turning his attention back to Ava again. "We won't be staying that long, sweetheart."

The stab of disappointment Megan felt was as unsettling as the goose bumps.

Focus, Megan. This is about the rescue, not you, she chided herself.

"Okay." She gave Tux's sleek head a reassuring pat. "I guess that's a good place to start."

Gage's attention shifted to Tux, but Megan saw his gaze linger on her arm for a moment. Ordinarily, she kept it covered but the temperature had risen as the day progressed and Megan had stripped off her flannel shirt, enjoying the warmth of the sunshine against her bare skin.

She'd never considered herself a vain person, yet suddenly Megan was battling the urge to cover the unsightly scar.

But Gage had already seen it…just like he'd seen each careful, halting step she'd taken the day they'd met.

"You and Tux are welcome to hop in the truck," Gage murmured. "There's plenty of room."

Megan knew he hadn't meant to imply that she wasn't capable of walking, but heat burned in her cheeks.

A project *and* an object of pity.

Neither one sat well with Megan even though she had a feeling Gage had meant well.

"Tux needs the exercise," she said lightly. "And it's a beautiful afternoon. We'll meet you there."

"Can I walk with them, Daddy?" Ava asked.

Gage looked at Megan and she nodded. "I don't mind."

Ava kept up a steady stream of chatter as they walked up the driveway, drowning out the cheerful song of the chickadees that flitted through the branches overhead.

Megan, who had more experience with canines than kids, tried to keep up with her cheerful monologue. Ava was a sweetheart. Curious and energetic, skipping into the woods to pluck a violet for Megan one moment and then gifting her with a shiny rock the next.

What had happened to the girl's mother?

It was one of the questions that had infiltrated Megan's thoughts over the course of the week.

She imagined that Gage would be quite the catch in a town the size of Pine Bridge. A successful businessman and good-looking, to boot.

But Megan recognized the signs of a workaholic. Based on the application he'd filled out, it was clear that Gage was stretching himself too thin.

She watched Ava chase after one of last autumn's oak leaves as it tumbled down the driveway, her lips moving to the words of a song no one else could hear.

How much time did Gage spend with his daughter? A few precious hours sandwiched between dinner and bedtime?

Not too long ago, Megan had been a lot like Gage. Her career had filled every nook and cranny of her life. Days off were spent in the gym, hiking trails, or on the bike path, strengthening body and mind to be successful.

Although the work Megan had done was important, she hadn't devoted time and attention to other things that mattered. Friends. Family.

And even though she hadn't known Gage very long, she was afraid he was making the same mistake.

Chapter Five

He'd offended her.

Gage mentally slapped himself upside the head as he waited beside the truck for Ava and Megan to return.

Not only had Megan caught him gawking at the scar on her arm, he'd implied that a short walk from the mailbox back to the house was too strenuous for her.

Gage was surprised she hadn't put him in his place. He might have, if the situation had been reversed.

In fact, more than anyone else, Gage understood what it was like to have people doubt your abilities. He'd heard his share of well-meaning comments after he'd returned to Pine Bridge.

Infants need round-the-clock care, Gage.

Being a single parent is tough. Are you sure you know what you're getting into?

How are you going to juggle a career and a newborn?

It had simply made Gage more determined to prove them wrong.

Yes, he'd only been twenty-two when Ava was born. Yes, long days and even longer nights had left Gage feeling like he was living final exam week every day. But he'd fallen in love with Ava the moment the nurse had placed her in his arms.

He couldn't believe Taylor hadn't fallen in love with

their daughter, too, but she'd been adamant that motherhood had never been one of her goals. *A mistake.* That's what she'd called Ava. And if Gage didn't support her decision to put their daughter up for adoption so they could go on with their lives, then being with him had been a mistake, too.

Gage had finally managed to convince Taylor to grant him full custody of Ava before she'd walked away without a backward glance. As far as mistakes went, Gage knew he would make his share. But bringing his infant daughter back to Pine Bridge hadn't been one of them.

"Daddy!" Ava broke through a gap in the trees, dried leaves clinging to her leggings, ponytail askew. She always ventured off the beaten path, searching for small treasures. "Look what I found!" She held up a bouquet of limp wildflowers for his inspection.

Nope. Gage wouldn't trade moments like these for anything.

"Wood violets," he said. "I think you found the first ones of the season."

Ava beamed and dashed back to Megan's side.

"Where's Baxter?" She looked around the yard for the dog.

"Taking an afternoon nap, but I'm sure he's ready to play now," Megan said. "Do you want to let him out?"

Ava nodded and scampered away, leaving the two of them alone.

"So…" Gage broke the silence. "What are your plans for the place?"

Megan's eyes lit up; a sign that he'd asked the right question this time.

While Ava and Baxter ran around the yard, Megan spent the next ten minutes sharing her vision for the rescue. There would be indoor-outdoor runs and a spacious fenced-in play yard to keep the dogs safe. A dog-washing/grooming station in one of the sheds that people from the community could use on a donation basis, with all the funds going back into the rescue.

"I'd like to have an open house at the end of May," Megan continued. "I want people to feel like Homeward Bound is part of the community."

Gage tried to conceal his reaction.

That was a little over a month away.

According to the note Mrs. Hayes had sent home, she wanted her students to volunteer a minimum of four hours to the Hearts and Hands project.

But looking around, Gage saw weeks, if not months, of hard work.

Baxter bounded up to them and sat down on his haunches, eyes intent as he stared at Megan.

"You must have worn him out, Aves." Gage chuckled as she joined them, breathless from the game of tag.

"It's five thirty," Megan said without glancing at her watch. "His internal dinner alarm goes off."

"I'm hungry, too," Ava informed him brightly.

Gage could see where this was going.

Did his daughter want to spend more time with Baxter?

Or Megan?

Gage didn't want to analyze his daughter's motives too closely. Nor did he want to analyze why the thought of sharing another dinner with Megan seemed more like an unexpected gift than another complication in his already complicated life.

He gave Ava's ponytail a gentle tug. "I'm glad you're hungry because it's dinnertime for us, too."

Gage didn't mention that tonight's menu involved stopping by the grocery store deli for a bucket of chicken and all the fixings.

He hadn't had time to grocery shop this week, either, a goal he'd planned to accomplish on the weekend.

"Can we come back tomorrow?" Ava wanted to know.

Gage mentally scrolled through his calendar. On Friday, he would be at a job site in the next county and had already asked Delaney Anderson, Willow's mom, if Ava could go home with them after school so the girls could play together until he got back.

But with Ava and Megan both waiting for his answer, Gage silently rearranged his schedule for the weekend and grocery shopping fell to the bottom of the list.

"How about Saturday morning?"

"Hey, big guy. Ready for your walk?"

Both Baxter and Tux perked up when they heard the W-word. Megan's newest guest, on the other hand, stared at her with soulful dark eyes and refused to budge from his crate.

Megan rocked back on her heels, at a loss as to what to do. Jac had been certain that CB would bounce back with a change in scenery and some loving, one-on-one attention, but Megan had had a difficult time coaxing him out of the kennel.

Tux whined and nudged Megan's shoulder. "I know. We have to be patient, though, buddy," she told him. "CB will come around, just like you did."

The difference was, Tux had been taken away from his previous owner because of neglect. CB's had passed away.

Megan dug into the pocket of her jeans and extracted a handful of bacon-flavored treats. CB's nose twitched and she held it out so he could see it. "One of these is yours."

Baxter yipped what was either an encouragement or an impatient reminder the new guy was holding up the show, but it had the desired effect. The Lab army-crawled out of the crate and delicately lipped the biscuit from Megan's palm.

"That wasn't so hard, was it?" she crooned. "Now, let's get some fresh air before our volunteers arrive."

A glance at the clock told Megan that would be in about fifteen minutes.

Gage had texted the night before to confirm their nine o'clock arrival time on Saturday morning, but Megan had already been awake for several hours, going through a mental checklist of what needed to be done. And, in what felt like an exercise in organizational triage, deciding which projects had to be tackled right away and which ones could wait.

Megan opened the door and the scent of last night's April shower still lingered. Along with the shallow puddles that Baxter and Tux happily splashed through as they set off down the driveway.

"Looks like fun, doesn't it?" Megan said to CB.

In response, the Lab flopped down on the grass.

Megan caught her lower lip between her teeth and knelt down to pet him. She'd call Jac again this afternoon with an update and ask her friend if she had any suggestions. CB had been tempted by the biscuit but the kibbles Megan had poured in his dish the night before had remained untouched.

The sound of a pickup rolling up the driveway told Megan that help had arrived.

Not only were Gage and Ava here, they were on time.

Megan rose to her feet. She expected the stab of pain in her knee. The butterflies that took wing in her stomach when Gage got out of the truck were something new.

In faded jeans, hiking boots and a long-sleeved T-shirt with the Triple L logo silk-screened on the front, he could have graced the cover of an outdoor magazine.

And she was staring again.

Megan tore her gaze away from him and focused on Ava. This morning, the little girl wore denim overalls over a T-shirt the same shade of cotton-candy pink as her cowboy boots. Her hair had been separated into two crooked braids, the ends secured and embellished with bows. The thought of Gage's large, work-roughened hands attempting such an intricate hairstyle had Megan hiding a smile.

"We're here!" Ava skipped up to Megan and once again, Megan found herself on the receiving end of an exuberant hug that also encompassed Tux, who'd sidled back to her when he'd heard the truck coming up the drive.

Megan hadn't realized how much she'd been looking forward to seeing Ava again.

And her father.

Megan shook that pesky thought away and returned Ava's hug.

Her eyes met Gage's over Ava's head and she managed to find her voice.

"Good morning."

"Morning." Gage's voice sounded husky, like he either needed a little more sleep or a little more coffee, and the butterflies took flight again.

Ava danced away and her eyes widened when she spotted CB in the grass. "You got another dog!"

"His name is CB and he's only staying with me for a few days," Megan explained. "Would you like to say hello?"

"Uh-huh!"

Megan had no idea if there had been children in CB's family, but maybe Ava's outgoing personality would draw the dog out of his shell a little.

Ava dropped down beside CB. "I'm Ava," she told him. "Me and my dad came over to help Miss Megan today. You can watch us if you want to."

CB sighed and rested his chin on his paws.

Ava's brow furrowed. "Is he sick?"

"No, but some dogs don't do well with change." Some people, either. "I'm sure Baxter would like to play with you, though." Megan pointed to the dog, who was standing several yards away, a rubber ball already clamped between his teeth.

The last two hours, Baxter had been camped out in front of the window, almost as if he'd been waiting for their neighbors to arrive.

Megan, tempted to do the same thing, had had to resist the urge to pull the curtains closed.

"Okay!" Ava brightened and ran over to him, just as eager to play.

Maybe instead of adopting another dog, Megan should adopt a six-year-old girl. Unlike her, Ava's energy level matched that of her canine companions.

"I put on a pot of coffee, if you'd like a cup before we start," she told Gage.

"Thank you, but I brought a thermos." He glanced at CB, no doubt wondering if dogs were going to continue to sprout in the yard like the wood violets Ava had picked the last time they were there. "Where do you want to start?"

"I'm not quite sure," Megan confessed. "I put together a list of the most pressing things, but it seems to keep changing."

"I know the feeling."

Megan wondered if he was referring to work in general or being drafted into helping Ava with a school project. Gage put in a lot of hours during the week so weekends were probably his time to catch up on things at home.

All the more reason not to take up any more of his time than necessary.

While Ava continued to play with Baxter, Megan shared the things she hoped to accomplish first.

"I've almost finished cleaning out the largest out-building," she told him. "Mr. McMurphy's family already took everything they wanted, so most of what's left will go straight into the dumpster."

"What about the broken window and the service door? Have you picked up replacements yet?"

Of course a builder would have noticed those things.

Megan wasn't sure whether she should be relieved or embarrassed by the amount of "fixing" that her fixer-upper actually required.

"Yes…" But the projects that involved heavy lifting were at the bottom of Megan's list. Both the window and the wooden door, stripped of paint and gnawed on by countless tiny critters seeking access to shelter over the years, fell into that category.

"Doors and windows are kind of my thing, you know," Gage said, almost as if he'd read her mind. "But if you'd rather I do something else, you're the boss. You call the shots here."

His quiet statement stirred gratitude in Megan's heart, as if he'd known it was difficult for her to admit her limitations.

"All right," Megan agreed. "Ava and I can measure and set up cones to outline the outdoor play area. I've left messages with several local handymen who advertise in the newspaper, but no one has called me back yet." Another setback Megan hadn't anticipated. "Ron, who works at the hardware store, mentioned there's more work than people willing to take on smaller projects like that."

Gage's nod confirmed that Ron had been telling the truth, but didn't explain the frown that settled between his brows. It wasn't his problem, though. Megan was already grateful for a few extra hands on a Saturday morning.

"No worries. I'll find someone." She had to.

Chapter Six

Guilt pricked Gage's conscience.

Because any "local handyman" with a reputation for quality and dependable service already worked for Triple L Builders. So, yeah. He was a little worried.

"I can give you some names," Gage heard himself say.

Megan couldn't hide her relief. "That would be great."

"Miss Megan!" Ava dashed up to them, Baxter lumbering along behind her. "What do you want me to do now?"

"You and I are going to decide how big to make the play yard for the dogs while your dad replaces a door." Megan pointed to the smaller shed. "That one is already empty, so I've been storing supplies in it," she told Gage. "There are some tools, too."

Gage grinned. "That's okay. I brought my own."

Megan grinned back and…was it his imagination or did she suddenly look more relaxed?

Gage always had a lengthy to-do list of his own on the weekends but suddenly he didn't mind setting it to the side to help Megan. Because it was the neighborly thing to do, of course.

Megan crossed the lawn and Gage found himself watching the way the sunlight picked out threads of gold in her hair, not the slight hitch in her step.

He pulled his gaze away.

Neighbors, he reminded himself sternly.

Time to get to work.

Over the next hour, Gage found his rhythm in what someone else might have considered the mundane. He removed the old casement window and ended up having to cut some boards to replace the ones that were rotten.

This was what he missed the most. His dad was the one who'd encouraged Gage to pursue a degree in architecture, but Gage loved working with his hands. Designing a home from scratch, seeing it come to life on the blueprints, didn't quite bring the same amount of satisfaction as helping set the walls in place, being there on site as it took shape from the ground up.

After Gage had taken the helm of Triple L, he'd spent the majority of his time in the office or on his phone in the truck, telling other people what to do.

Gage's cell phone began to ring and he managed to pry off another board while extricating it from his pocket.

Tom, the head of his roofing crew.

"Boss? We have a problem."

Not what Gage wanted to hear when he was in the middle of a project. "What's up?"

"I'm here with the guys, but we can't start yet."

"The shingles were delivered yesterday." Gage had checked.

"The storm that blew through last night took down a few trees." Tom paused, letting Gage fill in the blanks.

"How bad?"

"You tell me."

Gage wrestled down a sigh. "I'm in the middle of something but I can swing by and take a look. It'll be about twenty minutes, though."

"Appreciate it, boss."

Gage ended the call and stuck his phone in his back pocket.

Megan and Ava had moved to the grassy area on the other side of the shed, setting down orange cones to mark a square for the outdoor play yard. Tux and Baxter were camped out in a shady spot underneath a maple tree, snoozing while the humans worked.

Megan looked up and her smile arrowed through him, making what Gage had to say even more difficult. He'd blocked off three hours that morning to help Megan and running over to the job site would take a sizeable chunk from the allotted time.

"Hi, Daddy!" Ava waved when she spotted him, her cheeks kissed pink by the sun.

Gage glanced at Megan and saw her smile fade, as if she knew there was another reason he'd sought them out. "I'm sorry, but we have to go, Aves."

"Why?" Ava looked stricken. "We just got here!"

"My roofing crew ran into a problem and I have to meet them over at the job site and decide what to do," Gage explained.

"But we promised Miss Megan we'd help her!" Tears filled Ava's eyes, making Gage feel even worse.

"We can come back," he told her. "It shouldn't take more than an hour."

"But—"

"Ava can stay with me until you get back," Megan said.

Gage hadn't expected that.

Ava perked up instantly, though Gage wasn't sure he should take Megan up on the offer. He was already cutting out before barely making a dent in the project she'd assigned. Megan had her own list of things to accomplish. He didn't expect her to babysit, too.

"Really, Gage. If you're okay with it, we'll be fine," Megan assured him. "Ava is a great helper."

"Miss Megan showed me how to put the cones in a straight line, Daddy," Ava chimed in.

Under different circumstances, Gage would have smiled.

Working alone, Megan could have finished setting the boundaries of the play yard in half the amount of time, but it was clear that her patience extended to small children as well as her four-legged friends.

Gage gave in. "Listen to Miss Megan, okay? She's in charge."

"I will!" Ava promised.

"Sorry about this," Gage said again. "I'll be back as soon as I can."

Megan forced a smile.

"I understand."

All too well, unfortunately.

How many times had Megan apologized to her parents and siblings? Her grandma Lou? Put her name in for overtime shifts? Extra training? Thinking she had all the time in the world to spend time with them once she'd proven herself.

But then her world had come crashing down, literally, and Megan had vowed never to take those relationships for granted again.

She took a quick head count as Gage walked away and realized one dog was unaccounted for.

"Ava? Have you seen CB?"

The girl shook her head. "He was right over there." She pointed to a sunny spot in the grass.

Megan scanned the yard.

"CB!" She called his name, trying not to panic. The Lab was a senior and on the pudgy side. He couldn't have ventured too far away.

"Maybe you should whistle," Ava suggested.

Megan tried that, too. Baxter and Tux came loping over and Gage turned around.

"Was that for the dogs? Or me?" he called half teasingly.

"CB." Megan tried to smile back and failed. "He must have wandered off."

Without a moment's hesitation, Gage joined the search. He disappeared inside one of the outbuildings while Megan jogged back to the house to check the porch.

There was no sign of him.

Megan was officially panicking now.

She met up with Gage in front of the shed where he'd been working. He saw the question in her eyes and shook his head.

"Is anyone living over there that I can call? Maybe

he wandered that way." Megan pointed to the property that butted up against hers. She hadn't noticed a house, but that didn't mean there wasn't one there. A lot of people liked their privacy.

"Sorry, it's vacant land."

Megan's heart sank. How was she supposed to tell Jac she'd lost CB?

She wasn't the dog's owner. Could barely get CB to acknowledge her presence. Even if he was within hearing range, he might not respond to her voice.

"CB's a Lab, right?" Gage said. "He might have gone down to the creek."

Fear squeezed the air from Megan's lungs. "What creek?"

"It runs along the back of our properties."

Megan remembered seeing it on the map, but until she could trust herself to stay upright, hiking uneven ground to explore the perimeter of the property was something she hadn't tackled yet. The creek would be high this time of year from the newly melted snow and the spring rains, creating hazards in the way of deep pockets of loose ground between tree roots that weren't visible until you broke through the crust of mud and sank up to your knees.

"Is there a road back there?" Megan asked.

Gage shook his head. "A footpath on our side, but I don't think Neil ever went down there."

While Megan considered how likely it was that CB had been lured from the yard by the scent of water, Gage pivoted away from her and Ava and strode toward his truck.

Because his crew was waiting for him and they'd already spent twenty minutes searching for a runaway Lab.

"We'll see you later," Megan called after him. "I've got a whistle in the house. If he went down to the creek, he might hear it and come back."

Gage cast a disbelieving look over his shoulder.

"I'm not leaving. I'll take a quick look and see if he decided to go for a swim," he said. "I always keep an extra pair of muck boots in the truck, just in case."

Megan felt a little hand slip into hers.

"I'm worried about CB," Ava said in a small voice.

Megan didn't want to admit that she was, too...

"Megan?"

She looked up. Something in Gage's tone when he said her name stirred hope inside Megan.

He was standing next to his truck. The door was open. He grinned and pointed at something on the passenger side.

No. Way.

"You *found* him?"

Megan couldn't believe it.

Ava skipped along as Megan hurried over to the pickup. The window was down and she peered inside. CB sat on the leather seat, his tongue lolling in a happy doggy smile, and more alert than Megan had seen him since the day Jac had dropped him off.

"I didn't leave the door open," Gage told her.

She looked at the distance between the ground and the open window. "How..."

"Motivation?" Gage shrugged and motioned at the dog. "Okay, bud. Hide-and-seek is over."

CB didn't budge.

"I think he wants to go with you, Daddy." Ava giggled.

"Come on, CB." Megan dug a biscuit from her pocket. "How about a treat?"

CB's nose didn't even twitch when offered a bribe.

"Gage has to leave," Megan said. "Time to get down."

Gage was looking at the dog thoughtfully. "What's his story?"

"According to my friend, Jac, his owner died last month. No one in the family wanted to take CB in, so he ended up at the shelter. He wasn't doing very well there. Refused to eat. Wouldn't come out of his kennel to socialize with the other dogs. I was planning to call Jac this afternoon because CB has been the same way here. Until now, anyway."

Gage reached out and fondled one of the dog's velvety ears. "I don't mind if he rides along."

Once again, the man had surprised her. But maybe Gage realized that giving in was easier than coaxing CB to relinquish the territory he'd claimed.

"I'm not sure…" Megan hedged. "What if he chews up the upholstery?"

"Are you a danger to my leather seats?" Gage asked the dog.

CB barked.

"I guess that settles it." Gage grinned again and Megan felt the impact all the way down to her toes.

Talk about dangerous…

Gage swung his lean frame into the cab. "We'll be back."

Bemused, Megan watched the truck rattle down the driveway.

"Miss Megan?"

With a start, Megan realized that Ava had asked her a question.

"I'm sorry. What did you say?"

"I said that CB likes Daddy, doesn't he?"

"I think so." It seemed more likely the dog liked pickup trucks, but Megan didn't voice the thought out loud.

"Daddy is great," Ava said. "He's funny, too."

"Mmm-hmm."

"And he knows how to make pancakes."

"Pancakes are yummy."

"He lets me stay up late and watch movies sometimes, but not if it's a school night." Ava chattered on. "He knows all the words to the songs and sometimes he sings them when he's taking a show—"

"How about we take a little break after we finish our next project?" Megan interrupted, deciding it would be wise to steer the conversation in a different direction. "We can sit in the shade underneath that tree over there and have a snack and some lemonade."

Ava's eyes lit up. "Like a picnic."

"Like a picnic."

"Okay!" Two seconds of silence. And then… "Miss Megan?"

"Mmm?"

Ava tipped her head to one side, her eyes as bright and inquisitive as a chickadee's. "Have you ever gone camping?"

"Lots of times," Megan said. "Mostly when I was young, like you."

"Was it fun?"

"I enjoyed it." Megan smiled when Ava took hold of her hand again. "What about you?"

"Not yet." Ava flashed her signature smile. "But I think I like it, too."

Chapter Seven

"It must have come down during the storm last night, boss."

Gage stared at the massive branch that had split from the top of a white pine and impaled the roof of the brand-new home like an arrow that had found the center of the target.

His crew had agreed to work overtime on a Saturday to stay on schedule, but now the sizeable hole would have to be repaired before they could start.

"Can you get Eddie over here to fix it today?"

"Sorry." Tom shook his head. "He's out of town visiting his grandkids."

Gage blew out a sigh and mentally adjusted his schedule again. "I'll take care of it tomorrow after church then."

He'd have to ask Delaney if Ava could spend the afternoon with her and Willow again. Delaney was a single parent, too, although she shared an apartment above The Three Chocolatiers with her aunt Hope, who owned the business. Delaney never seemed to mind an impromptu playdate. Had, in fact, encouraged Gage to let her know if he had a meeting or got tied up at work. The two girls got along extremely well, but Gage was careful not to take advantage of Delaney's generous offer unless it was a true emergency.

Lately, it seemed like Gage had had more than his share.

It suddenly occurred to him that Delaney's name wasn't on Ava's list. Willow's mom had moved in with Hope only a year ago, so Gage didn't know her story, but it struck him as odd that Ava hadn't considered that if he and Delaney got together, she would get a mom *and* a sister.

"I can get up there and help you." Tom was still contemplating the branch as he scratched at the salt-and-pepper bristles sprouting from his chin. "Me and Brenda don't have anything else going on tomorrow except sitting on the deck and soaking up some sun."

That was why Gage shook his head. Brenda, Tom's wife, had just finished her third and, please God, last, chemo treatment. A leisurely afternoon with nothing to do was exactly what the couple needed.

"It looks like a one-man job," Gage fibbed. "You just be back here bright and early on Monday morning."

"You don't need us?"

The question had Gage turning around to face the rest of the crew. Arch. Patrick. Ryan. All single, twentysomethings eager to make some overtime pay on the weekend. Now the trio looked as disappointed as a baseball team who'd just been informed their game had gotten rained out.

A thought struck him and a slow smile drew up the corners of Gage's lips.

"I wouldn't say that. I need some fencing put up today."

Arch nodded at the truck. "For your dog?"

Gage glanced over his shoulder. He'd almost forgotten about CB. The Lab had commandeered the driver's seat now, proudly sitting behind the steering wheel like he was about to drive off and leave Gage behind in a cloud of dust.

Good thing he'd taken the keys.

"He's not mine…he belongs to my neighbor." Kind of. Gage didn't bother to explain. The roofing crew would get their overtime and Megan's rescue dogs would get their outdoor play yard. "After you get that branch out of the roof and put a tarp over the hole, head over to the old McMurphy place."

The guys didn't even have to discuss it. Smiles broke out across their faces.

"You heard the boss." Tom jerked his head in the direction of the enclosed trailer. "Grab a ladder."

Gage opened the door of his pickup but he didn't have to scold or cajole to get his seat back. CB hopped over the center console with the agility of a six-month-old pup, then turned a circle before settling back down on the passenger seat with a contented sigh.

Megan and Ava were nowhere in sight when Gage returned. He swung down from the cab and opened the door for CB. The dog wouldn't budge again.

"You can't stay here. You know that, right?" Gage told him.

CB ignored the question and focused his attention on the tools that littered the floor mat, proving that six-year-olds weren't the only ones with selective hearing.

Gage let the dog have his way for now and made

sure all the windows were rolled down so air could circulate through the cab. A breeze filtered through the trees and the temperature remained on the cooler side in the morning, so he wasn't worried about the dog getting overheated.

He walked up the driveway, half expecting an ambush from Baxter with every step.

No sign of the dog, either.

Gage heard a distinctive giggle behind the outbuilding Megan had designated for the kennels and pivoted in that direction. He rounded the corner and spotted Ava and Megan sitting on a quilt underneath one of the sugar maples that formed a natural hedge at the edge of the property.

Tux, of course, had his head resting on the blanket near Megan's knee while Baxter was sitting as close to Ava as possible without being in her lap.

They hadn't noticed him yet, so Gage stopped, absorbing the sound of another giggle as his daughter responded to something Megan had said.

Gage had thought Taylor had done irreparable damage to his heart, but suddenly it was beating in double-time, reminding him it was still there. But that didn't mean there was enough left to give away.

And why had that thought even crossed his mind?

Gage began to back up, slowly, seeking refuge in the shed, where he would be in his element. Building. Repairing. It's what Gage excelled at. He'd built a life in Pine Bridge after Taylor left and he wouldn't put himself…or his daughter…at risk again.

"Daddy!" Ava had spotted him and waved her napkin in the air. "We're over here!"

Leaving him with no choice but to join them.

"You're having a tea party?" Gage's gaze skimmed over two small enamelware cups and a matching speckled red-and-white plate filled with slices of cheese and fresh fruit.

"It's not tea." Ava held it up for his inspection. "It's lemonade and we're camping."

"It's our reward for sweeping out the little shed," Megan said. "How did it go at the building site?"

"Roof zero, branch one." Gage reached for a ripe strawberry and popped it into his mouth.

"Will it throw you off schedule?" Megan asked.

Gage shook his head. "It's under control."

"Miss Megan maked banana bread, Daddy. Do you want some?"

She baked, too.

Gage's mouth instantly watered but he ignored it.

There was nothing wrong with the stuff he bought at the grocery store.

Nothing wrong with it being just the two of them. In fact, that was the way Gage wanted it. Ava might think she wanted a mom but they were doing just fine.

Even though Gage's idea of an impromptu picnic involved a cheese stick and juice box.

Even though watching Ava and Megan interact had him thinking about taking a little more time to laugh. To savor life instead of meeting his next goal.

"I'm going to start on that door." And put some distance between Megan and his rogue thoughts. "CB is still in the truck, by the way."

"I should get back to work, too." Megan rose to her feet. "I'll try and lure him out first, though. I keep some special treats in reserve for situations like this." She smiled at Ava. "I've never met a dog that can resist the smell of bacon."

Gage was finding it difficult to resist Megan's smile.

Ava and the two dogs trailed behind them as they crossed the lawn toward the shed. A pickup truck hauling a trailer was rolling up the driveway and Megan stopped, shaded her eyes against the sun.

"I wonder who that is. I'm not expecting a delivery today."

Gage smiled as the guys piled out of the pickup.

"I asked them to come over."

Megan blinked. "Why?"

"They're going to put up your fence."

Megan pulled into the parking lot of Pine Bridge Community, a small church on the outskirts of town with stained-glass windows and an old-fashioned steeple.

It was the first time since moving to Pine Bridge that Megan had attended a service. The moment she walked through the heavy double doors, an elderly couple greeted her, pointed to the carafes of coffee underneath a bulletin board, and encouraged her to stay after the service for their monthly potluck.

Megan helped herself to a cup of coffee and slipped inside the sanctuary.

There were wooden pews instead of chairs and a vase of daffodils adorned the keyboard on a raised platform at the front of the church.

And even though it looked nothing like the church Megan had attended before, she felt instantly at home.

A middle-aged man sitting near the front waved to her and Megan recognized Ron from the hardware store. A woman with a silver bob and funky red glasses smiled up at Megan as she approached.

"Good morning," Ron said cheerfully. "This is Connie, my better half. Connie, this is the young woman who's been single-handedly funding our next vacation with all her purchases."

The woman's blue eyes twinkled. "And I thank you for that. Ron and I haven't taken a vacation for twenty years."

"I'm happy to help." Megan grinned and stretched out her hand. "Megan Albright."

Connie blinked. "Megan... Albright? The woman with the dog rescue?"

"Yes. How did—"

"Miss Megan!"

Megan turned at the sound of the lilting voice and saw Ava skipping down the center aisle toward her.

A smile struggled to break free as Megan noticed the girl's ensemble this morning included a sparkly tutu layered over her leggings, a slightly lopsided tiara, and the pink cowboy boots.

Connie's eyes went wide when Ava hugged her.

"It looks like you two already know each other."

"We had kitchen sink pizza and I played with Baxter while Daddy helped Miss Megan fix her windows," Ava said, condensing the time they'd spent together. "And we're going over to her house again today!"

They were?

Gage hadn't mentioned it, but Megan felt that uptick in her pulse again.

"Really?" Connie looked fascinated by the information and Megan wasn't sure why.

"Uh-huh. Daddy says we can adopt a puppy, but I wouldn't mind a big dog like Baxter. He's a Funnyland."

Ron scratched the bald spot on his head. "Never heard of that breed before."

"I think she means Newfoundland."

Gage had walked up behind them and Megan's breath stalled in her lungs. She'd thought the man looked good in the standard issue T-shirt and faded jeans, but in gray cargo pants, a striped button-down that outlined his broad shoulders, and his hair still damp from a recent shower, he cleaned up pretty well on a Sunday morning, too.

"Good morning, boss." Connie almost sang the words and Gage's eyes narrowed. She ignored him and looked at Megan. "I know, I know. Most people want to avoid the people they work with on the weekend, but mine happens to come with an adorable side-kick—" she smiled at Ava "—so what are you going to do?"

"You work together?" Megan's gaze bounced from Connie to Gage and back again.

"I'm the office manager," Connie said. "The one

who is supposed to know everything that's going on."
She cast a meaningful look at Gage before giving Ron
a nudge. He dutifully slid down to make more room
and Connie patted the empty spot next to her on the
pew. "It'll be cozy but we'll all fit!"

"Cozy" wasn't the word Megan would have chosen. It must not have been Gage's, either, because he
reached out and took Ava by the hand.

"I'm helping with the offering," Gage said. "It's…
ah, easier, if we sit in the back row."

Connie looked disappointed but the worship team
had taken their places up front and the opening notes
of "Amazing Grace" began to waft through the sanctuary.

Megan released a silent breath, closed her eyes, her
heart finding its rhythm again as everyone around her
rose and began to sing.

God's faithfulness. His goodness.

Megan had struggled with both after the accident.
As a firefighter, she'd woken up every day knowing
what she was supposed to do. Her life had had meaning. Purpose.

And, yes, Megan had lost her way for a while. She'd
been confused. Angry. She'd even stopped reaching
out to God for answers but He hadn't stopped reaching out to her.

Grace.

It *was* pretty amazing.

After the service, Megan turned to the couple next
to her while a group of teens exited the row across
the aisle.

"It was nice meeting you, Connie." Megan's smile expanded to include Ron. "And I'm sure I'll see you at the hardware store this week. I'm going to need some more paint."

"You have to stay for the potluck!" Connie looked at her askance. "The food is delicious and there's plenty to go around."

"And you don't want to miss out on Connie's famous lemon meringue pie," Ron interjected. "I wouldn't get a piece if she didn't make two and leave one at home. It's always the first thing that disappears on the dessert table."

Connie swatted his arm but she looked pleased by the compliment. "It's a good way to get to know people. People who like dogs."

"I don't know." Megan was torn. The boys would be ready to stretch their legs and she was anxious to tackle the next item on her to-do list. The finished play yard had encouraged her that this new dream was closer to becoming a reality.

"Gage and Ava always stay," Connie added, the now-familiar twinkle returning to her eyes.

The thought of spending more time with her neighbors was more tempting than the lemon meringue pie.

Except, Megan wasn't sure if Gage would feel the same way.

Other than a few questions about the placement of a light fixture in the shed, Gage hadn't spoken to her much after he'd returned from the job site. And he'd left before his crew had finished the fence.

It almost felt like he'd been avoiding her, although Megan wasn't sure why.

Connie was suddenly surrounded by a group of women asking for details about a concert in the park. Megan eased around them and made her way out of the sanctuary.

The enticing aromas seasoning the air supported Connie's claim that the food would be delicious.

Megan sidestepped a young couple with a baby and spotted Gage talking to a slender woman with copper hair outside the fellowship hall. Her sleeveless sundress with its brightly colored patchwork skirt and uneven hemline had a vintage, second-hand-store type vibe that paired well with the jeweled butterfly clips in her hair and the strappy leather sandals on her feet.

Ava and another little girl who looked the same age skipped up to the couple, both talking a mile a minute, their expressions animated.

The woman leaned closer to Gage, her hand resting briefly on his arm, a casual gesture that told Megan they knew each other well. She said something that made him laugh before they turned and walked into the fellowship area together.

Megan's heart sank a little as she turned toward the doors in the opposite direction.

No matter what Ava had said about them coming over again that afternoon, it was clear Gage had other plans.

Chapter Eight

"The girls are playing in Willow's room." Delaney opened the door and ushered Gage inside the apartment she shared with her aunt. "I've got a pitcher of iced tea. Do you have a minute?"

Gage tried to hide his surprise. He was grateful Delaney had agreed to watch Ava while he spent Sunday afternoon patching the hole in the roof, but it was the first time she'd invited him inside after a scheduled playdate. As impossible as it seemed given how close Willow and Ava were, he hoped it didn't mean the girls hadn't been getting along.

"Sure." Gage followed Delaney into the kitchen off the living room. The upper apartment was more spacious than it looked from the street.

Delaney retrieved another glass from the cupboard and filled it before topping off her own. She didn't seem in a hurry to break the silence, so Gage did.

"What happened?"

Delaney hesitated. And blushed.

Oh, boy.

What could Ava possibly have said or done to make the ordinarily unflappable Delaney Anderson blush?

The answer to that could be just about anything. Six-year-olds weren't known for their tact.

"There's something I think you should know and, well…this is a little awkward."

Gage inwardly braced himself. "If it involves Ava, you have to tell me, Del."

"You know Johanna Waverly? Miranda and Stephen's daughter? She's in Ava and Willow's class."

"I think so." To be honest, Gage didn't pay a lot of attention to individual faces when he picked up Ava after school. All he saw was a pink stampede from the doors to the pickup area.

"A few days ago, I got an invitation from Miranda. She invited Willow and some of Johanna's friends on an outing next month. Miranda's parents own the campground on Derby Lake but it doesn't officially open until Memorial Day so they'll have the whole place to themselves.

"There's going to be campfire sing-alongs and games, and everyone is spending the night. The invitation describes it as a Glampout because Miranda hired a local artist to teach the girls how to make suncatchers and Nita, one of the moms who works at the salon, is going to do hair and nails."

"Sounds like fun," Gage said. Only because he felt like he should. "I'm surprised Ava hasn't mentioned it."

Delaney simply looked at him.

And...

Wow. The dots connected.

"Ava isn't *invited*?"

"It's on Mother's Day weekend, so Miranda invited all the girls' moms, too," Delaney said. "I feel terrible, Gage. I overheard Ava and Willow talking about it before you got here."

"Was Ava very upset?"

"Just the opposite."

Gage would have thought that was a good thing but, for some reason, Delaney's expression told him that no, it wasn't.

"They asked me for blankets to practice setting up a tent and Ava seems just as excited about it as Willow."

He raked his hand through his hair. He wanted to be angry. But this was life. It wasn't as if Miranda Waverly had intended to exclude anyone, but this was a mom-and-daughter event and Ava didn't have a mom.

"Ava isn't invited to every party," Gage murmured. "Maybe she won't mind missing out on this one."

"I heard Willow tell Ava that she can only go if she has a mom—I'm really sorry about that, but you know how blunt kids are—and…this is the awkward part."

Really? Gage thought they'd already gotten past it when Delaney had informed him that Ava hadn't received an invitation to her classmate's party.

"Ava said she'll have one by then."

That explained Delaney's blush. She must have assumed Ava had been referring to *her*.

Gage's neck suddenly felt warm.

Sure, Delaney was single. Pretty, too. But it had never crossed his mind to ask her out on a date.

In his mind's eye, Gage saw an enamelware pitcher and two metal cups on a quilt underneath the tree.

We're camping, Daddy, Ava had said.

He shook his head to dispel the image.

Because it meant that Megan had officially moved to the top of Ava's list.

* * *

"I'm really sorry, Megs, but I'm not going to be able to pick up CB for a few more days. The sheriff's department is transferring some animals that were being neglected to the local shelter, and because the vet clinic partners with them, we'll be doing the health screens."

Megan trapped the phone between her ear and shoulder blade as she straightened the pillows on the sofa. "I don't mind. It's not like he's a flight risk." Unless she counted him stowing away in Gage's truck.

"I did find out a little more about CB, though," Jac continued. "His owner's older sister turned in all the vet records when she surrendered him, and he's eleven years old. She also mentioned that Walt and CB were inseparable."

Megan glanced at the dog. She'd managed to coax him out of his kennel to go for a walk with Baxter and Tux, but as soon as they were back in the house, he'd retreated to his kennel.

"She couldn't take him in?"

"It didn't sound like it. She lives in a no-pets condo in Phoenix and only came back to Wisconsin to settle the estate. I got the impression the siblings weren't close. Walt was a long-distance truck driver and never had a family of his own. It sounds like CB was his best friend."

Megan had a feeling that went both ways.

Her heart ached for the dog.

"I know you aren't set up for another dog yet so I'll get there as soon as I can," Jac continued. "How's it going, by the way? Did anyone get back to you about the fence yet?"

"Actually…it's finished."

"*Finished?*" Jac echoed. "The last time I talked to you, you were having trouble getting anyone to return your calls. How did that happen?"

"Gage Lawrence's roofing crew came over yesterday. They finished the whole thing by midafternoon." Megan still walked over to the window every so often to make sure she hadn't been dreaming.

A pause. And then, "Who is Gage Lawrence?"

It was a simple question that Megan didn't know quite how to answer.

"He's a local builder and he lives next door."

"A builder? Wow." Jac chuckled. "I guess your prayers were answered and then some."

Megan felt herself blushing and she was glad Jac couldn't see her face. Her best friend could be as tenacious as the German shepherds she trained for a private security firm in her spare time.

She should have known her silence would give her away.

"Why aren't you agreeing with me?" Jac asked suspiciously. "Is the guy a jerk or something?"

"No," Megan said quickly. "He…"

Again. Simple question. Not so simple answer.

"Is so attractive he leaves you speechless?" Jac teased.

"Can we talk about something else?"

The squeal on the other end of the line made Megan wince.

"He *is* attractive. I knew it! And you're blushing, aren't you?"

Megan pressed a palm against her cheek. "Yes. He's attractive, okay? Moving on."

"Available?" Jac didn't move on.

Megan remembered the pretty redhead smiling up at Gage outside the fellowship room. "I have no idea. What I do know is that he's a workaholic, just like I was."

"But he didn't have to send his roofing crew over to put up the fence," Jac pointed out.

"There's an ulterior motive. He wants me to be able to house more dogs so he can adopt one."

"He could afford one of those non-shedding designer breeds and wants a rescue?" Jac's sigh was the same one Megan heard at the conclusion of their monthly rom-com marathons.

"His daughter, Ava, is the animal lover. And before you ask, he's a single dad."

"The plot thickens."

"I'm saying goodbye now—"

"You claim not to know anything about him, so let me help you out." Jac ignored her. "Gage Lawrence owns his own business. He paid his crew to finish your fence in an afternoon. He's a good dad. He's single. Oh…and he's attractive, too—"

"Gotta go. Love ya."

She ended the call with Jac's laughter ringing in her ear.

Monday mornings had a rep for a reason.

Gage had already received voice mails from the

heads of two different crews on the drive to school, and then, when he'd turned into the parking lot, Ava went into panic mode as she'd realized she'd forgotten her lunch. Gage had placed a kiss on her head, promised he would drop it off, and headed back home.

The buds on the trees had unfurled thanks to last week's rain and warmer temperatures. Gage rolled down the window, letting the fragrant spring air infiltrate the cab.

But what he smelled was…smoke.

Gage's heart slammed against his ribs. He cranked the steering wheel, gravel churning as he changed directions and turned down Megan's driveway.

A dozen scenarios chased through Gage's mind and every single one of them chilled him to the bone. Especially when he saw the skeins of dark smoke hanging over the shed.

He slammed the truck into Park and vaulted from the cab.

There was no sign of the dogs or Megan.

"Megan!"

He rounded the shed, phone in hand just in case he had to call for backup, and pulled up short.

A fire was blazing in the center of the yard, but Megan stood a few feet away from it, not helpless or in distress, but calmly sipping coffee from a stainless-steel mug.

"What…?" The word came out in a wheeze. Gage was feeling a little light-headed. He hadn't sprinted like that since his last track meet in high school.

Megan's eyes went wide. "Gage? Is everything all right?"

"That's…what I was about to ask you."

She tipped her head, confusion replacing her concern. "Is there a reason it wouldn't be?"

"I saw the smoke and…"

Understanding dawned in the violet-blue eyes. And then she laughed.

Laughed.

Even though Gage didn't see anything the least bit funny about scaring a decade off his life.

She pressed her fingers against her lips while she regained control, but Gage could still see the amusement dancing in her eyes.

"You were worried about me?"

Well. Sure. They were neighbors.

Even though he hadn't been acting like it.

Gage hadn't sought out Megan after the worship service on Sunday. Hadn't scheduled any more Hearts and Hands work days after Delaney had dropped the bombshell about Ava having a mom by the weekend of the campout.

"There's a ban on campfires in the county this time of year," Gage muttered.

"It was lifted two days ago," Megan said. "I know what I'm doing, Gage. I'm… I was a firefighter before I moved to Pine Bridge."

Megan could tell Gage hadn't been expecting her to say that, but he recovered quickly.

"A firefighter." He shook his head. "Now I feel like an idiot, coming to your rescue."

Megan was touched by his concern. And having Gage Lawrence charge up her driveway in his shiny silver pickup to check on her was kind of sweet.

"There were some old pallets in the shed that I wanted to get rid of," she told him. "This seemed like the quickest, most efficient way to do it."

"What else is on your list for today?"

Gage seemed genuinely interested, so Megan shared the top three. "Now that the fencing is up, I'm going to clean out the last shed and call around to find a plumber to hook up the washing station. I have to respond to some emails, too. I've already heard from the directors of several shelters that are maxed out, asking if I have room."

"How many will you take in?"

"I should be able to handle three at a time."

He looked surprised. "Counting your own?"

Megan shook her head. "In addition to. Bax and Tux are house dogs. The rescues will have all the comforts of home out here."

Baxter, who'd discovered a patch of sunshine a few yards away, cracked open his eyes when she'd said his name. Tux, who was as suspicious of smoke as Gage, had positioned himself a safe distance away from the burning pallets.

Gage's cell began to ring and Megan saw the flash of indecision on his face. "Go ahead and answer it," she told him. "I know you have a list today, too."

Gage answered and ended the call in less than fifteen seconds. Megan expected him to jump back in the truck but he looked at the house instead.

"How is CB doing?"

"I left the door of his kennel open but other than our first walk of the morning, he hasn't ventured out yet."

"I'm driving up to a new job site north of here today," Gage said. "He can ride along with me."

Megan struggled to hide her shock. "Really?"

Gage shrugged. "Why not? He didn't chew up my upholstery the last time. I did get the feeling if I left the keys in the ignition, he'd drive away without me, though."

Megan chuckled. She wasn't sure she'd be able to coax the dog out of his kennel but it was worth a try.

She took the shovel and used it to push the glowing embers into the pile. Stripped off her gloves and tucked them into her back pocket.

"Let's find out."

Tux attached himself to Megan's side as they walked up to the house while Baxter ambled next to Gage.

Gage pulled up short as they entered the house. "You're baking again." He said the words almost accusingly.

"Cinnamon rolls." Megan nodded at the glass pan

next to the coffeepot in the kitchen. "You can take some along, if you'd like."

"No way," Gage said instantly. "I almost had a mutiny on my hands after the crew got a taste of those chocolate-chip cookies on Saturday. Arch wanted to know if you were looking for a permanent crew."

Megan smiled. "I bake when I can't sleep."

Gage's brows dipped together and she wished she could take the words back. Megan didn't want him to feel sorry for her.

She walked over to the kennel and carefully lowered herself to the floor. "Hey, CB. Look who's here."

Gage knelt beside her and the scent of the outdoors and some masculine soap teased Megan's senses. He stretched out his hand. "Hey, buddy. Got any big plans for the day?"

"Come on out," Megan coaxed, fishing in her pocket for a biscuit—which CB ignored.

"I appreciate the offer, Gage, but—"

"Truck?" he said to CB.

Megan lost her balance and almost toppled over as the Lab burst from the opening of the kennel like a furry cannonball.

Gage chuckled. "I guess I figured out the password."

Megan awkwardly righted herself, pretending she hadn't noticed Gage's outstretched hand as she stood up. "I guess you did. It makes sense, though. Jac told me that his owner was a long-distance driver and they went everywhere together until CB was dropped off at the shelter."

"Ah. Now the name makes sense." Gage knuckled the dog's head.

"It does?"

"CB? Citizens Band radio? The way truckers used to communicate when they were on the road."

Megan looked at him in bemusement. "I'll take your word for that."

Gage fished his keys from the pocket of his jeans and CB's tail began to slash the air. "I'll bring him home later today, if that's okay."

It was more than okay. It fell under the category of another God surprise.

Gage Lawrence owns his own business. He paid his crew to finish your fence in an afternoon. He's a good dad. He's single. Oh...and he's attractive, too.

Jac's teasing voice echoed in Megan's mind.

There was something else Megan could add to the list now.

The man was unpredictable.

Just when Megan thought she had Gage all figured out, he did something totally unexpected.

But unpredictable was risky and Megan no longer lived for the adrenaline rush. She wanted stability. Wanted to take time and savor the world instead of trying to conquer it.

Like Gage.

So. Yes. Even though God might have brought Gage into her life to help her dream become a reality, it didn't mean she was going to let herself dream about *him*.

Something she had to remind herself of at least a hundred times over the course of the day.

* * *

CB was missing again.

Gage opened the door and stared at the empty passenger seat in disbelief.

How…

He'd stopped by the supply building to pick up some stain samples for one of the unfinished houses, expecting CB would sit tight until he got back. Gage had had to coax him outside for some quick stretch breaks but, over the past six hours, the dog had been the epitome of canine decorum as long as he could view the world from the cab of the pickup.

Gage looked around. His watch beeped a reminder that school would be letting out for the day in fifteen minutes. And since it was a seven-minute drive to the elementary school, that left Gage with eight minutes to figure out what had prompted CB to go AWOL on him.

A feminine laugh wafted from the window of the main office building and Gage frowned.

Maybe it hadn't been a what. Maybe it had been a *who*.

Connie looked up when he opened the door. Sure enough. She was sitting on the floor next to CB, who was sprawled out like a furry rug in front of her desk. But how had his office manager convinced the dog to leave his happy place?

"You didn't tell me you'd adopted a dog!"

"He's not…" Gage leveled an accusing stare at CB. "Cheetos? Really? That's your kryptonite?"

The evidence—a smudge of orange dust glowing on

CB's muzzle—disappeared with one efficient swipe of his tongue.

"I'm sure Ava is over the moon," Connie continued. "I have to admit I was shocked when she told us that you were going to add another member to the Lawrence family."

Gage's imagination momentarily took control of his thoughts and pictures of Megan flashed in front of his eyes. Laughing with Ava. Snuggled up on the sofa next to him…

He yanked them back in line.

"I'm only taking care of him for the day," he told her. And not very well, if he could lose track of an eighty-pound Lab in less than five minutes. "He likes trucks."

And Cheetos, apparently.

"Mmm." Connie smiled. He could practically *see* the wheels turning in her head. "Ava seems to be taken with Megan. She mentioned pizza…and helping out at the rescue."

Gage shouldn't have been surprised that his daughter had managed to download all that information in the sixty-second head start she'd had as they'd entered the sanctuary on Sunday morning. It also didn't surprise him that Connie wanted to know what, if anything, was going on between Gage and their new neighbor. More than once, she'd lamented about his lack of a social life.

"Ava chose the rescue as a school project, so we're putting in some volunteer hours there. And speaking of that… We have to get on the road or I'll be late picking her up from school."

"If Megan needs volunteers, I'll pass that information on to the youth pastor. He's always looking for ways to get the kids involved in the community. I have no idea what brought her to our little town, but we want her to stay."

Gage ignored the slight emphasis on the word "we."

He wasn't sure what had brought Megan to Pine Bridge, either, but after their conversation that morning, he had a hunch it had more to do with the fact she was no longer a firefighter than finding the perfect piece of property for the rescue.

She'd come to Pine Bridge to start over, just like he had.

And starting over could be a scary thing.

It had worked out for Gage, though. He had a good life.

A busy life, as Megan had pointed out. One he'd thought looked great on paper.

But for some reason, his six-year-old daughter had read between the lines and decided there was something missing.

And, lately, in spite of Gage's inner pep talks that things were fine, an intriguing young woman with a nurturing heart and a beautiful smile was making Gage wonder the same thing.

Megan heard a truck coming up the driveway and the breath she'd been holding for most of the day emptied out of her lungs.

They were back.

Baxter's ears lifted and then he launched to his feet. He was already halfway across the lawn before he glanced over his shoulder at Megan to make sure she was a member of the greeting party.

Gage pulled up next to the outbuilding and Megan could see CB sitting proudly on the seat beside him, looking as if he belonged there.

And when Ava popped out of the back seat and Gage hopped down from the cab in dust-covered boots and a Triple L Builders polo…well, it looked as if they belonged, too.

Right here.

The thought stole Megan's breath all over again.

How had her neighbors worked their way into her heart so quickly?

She tried to tell herself that she was grateful for their help. But gratitude alone didn't account for the joy that welled up inside Megan when Ava hugged her.

"We brought CB back!"

Megan's eyes met Gage's over her head. "I see that. How was he?"

"Only lost him once."

Gage spoke the words matter-of-factly but Megan couldn't tell if he was teasing or not.

He opened the door and, to her astonishment, the dog immediately jumped down from the cab.

"How…?" Megan blinked.

"Trucks are first in his heart unless Cheetos are involved. You may want to pick up a bag the next time you go to the store."

CB trotted over and greeted both Baxter and Tux, acknowledging their presence for the first time since he'd arrived.

And all because Gage had brought the dog along with him to work.

"Was Ava surprised when she saw CB?" Megan asked.

"Surprised?" Gage's low laugh rumbled through the air. "She practically teleported from the sidewalk to the truck when she spotted him."

"I smell smoke." Ava released Baxter and stood up, her pert nose wrinkling as she sniffed the air.

"Megan is just burning some scrap wood," Gage said. "Nothing to be worried about."

But he'd been worried. And the memory of him rounding the corner, ready to save her from disaster, had been enough to ward off the chill of the spring morning even without a fire.

"I switched to firewood after the pallets were gone," Megan confessed. "I love the smell of a campfire, so I kept it going. I'm thinking I might cook my dinner outside tonight."

"Outside?" Ava looked delighted at the thought.

"Nothing fancy. Just hot dogs and campfire potatoes."

Megan had Ava's full attention now. "We cooked marshmallows once when Grandpa lived with us. Mine turned black so Daddy made me another one."

Before Megan could stop them, the words slipped out.

"I have plenty to go around, if you'd like to stay."

Ava whirled toward Gage, her expression hopeful, and, too late, Megan realized she'd put him on the spot. She suddenly remembered his rather abrupt departure on Saturday. And the red-haired woman he'd been deep in conversation with outside the fellowship room after church.

"You aren't obligated to feed us, you know," Gage said. "Contrary to what Ava claims, I do know how to cook."

"Consider it a thank you for taking CB with you today," Megan said.

"Then we accept."

When Gage smiled, Megan realized she didn't feel obligated at all. From the moment she'd watched his truck drive away early that morning, this was how she'd hoped the day would end.

Chapter Ten

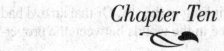

"She's going to sleep good tonight." Gage watched Ava zigzag through the grass, chasing one of the fireflies that had appeared just after sunset.

"So will Baxter." Megan poked one of the logs with a stick and sent a shower of sparks into the air. "Ready for another marshmallow?"

Gage groaned and patted his stomach. "No thanks. If I eat any more, I'm going to turn into one."

He couldn't believe they'd stayed this long. Ordinarily, on a school night, they had a routine. Ava would take a bath and play with her toys while Gage cleaned up the kitchen and dealt with the emails that inevitably popped up in his inbox after the office had officially closed for the day.

Yet tonight, Gage was in no hurry to go home. Tonight, he wasn't counting the minutes until he could turn the lights off and fall into bed.

Megan had claimed that her campfire supper would be simple and it was. There'd been hot dogs, a bowl of fresh strawberries, and crispy potato wedges fried in the cast-iron skillet she'd placed over the tripod. The menu might have been limited but the food was delicious. But that wasn't the reason Gage had lingered at the campfire long after they'd eaten.

It was the company.

Gage hadn't known the fireflies almost outnumbered the stars winking in the sky. Or that an owl had taken up residence in the woods between the properties.

But sitting with Megan, he was cognizant of all the little things that would have slipped past him in his haste to "do the next thing."

She reached for a piece of kindling to add to the fire and the next thing Gage knew, Megan was sprawled on the grass.

He helped her back into the chair, his heart hammering in his chest even though they were sitting a safe distance away from the fire.

"Sorry." Megan winced. "I try to do things but my body doesn't always cooperate."

His gaze moved to her arm and he could picture the angry scar underneath the sleeve of her hoodie.

It was hard enough to wrap his head around the fact that Megan had entered burning buildings on purpose. But if she was living here in Pine Bridge instead of Eau Claire, it could only mean that her injuries had been significant enough to end her career.

Gage felt his cell phone vibrate in his coat pocket and ignored it. "What happened?"

The question arrowed through Megan and found the tender places inside that hadn't quite healed yet.

She'd grown accustomed to people averting their gazes, politely avoiding her scars. Talking about everything but the job she'd loved.

The other firefighters were like family yet they'd avoided talking about it, too. Like them, Megan had been trained and capable and strong, and the accident had happened anyway.

She'd done everything to reduce the number of risks, but she was a reminder that the very nature of the job was fraught with them. And although her fellow fighters had been nothing but supportive, being that reminder was one of the reasons Megan had decided to move.

"I'm sorry," Gage muttered. "It's none of my business."

Megan realized she didn't mind talking about the accident. But until now, until Gage, no one had asked.

"I'd taken on an extra shift that weekend when a call came in that a single-family residence was on fire. One of the neighbors saw fire coming out of the chimney and said there was a couple with two children living there."

In her mind's eye, Megan relived that moment. By the time they'd arrived, smoke was pouring out of the windows.

"Thanks to the neighbor, the parents and their ten-year-old son had gotten out, but the mother was hysterical. When they'd gone into their four-year-old daughter's bedroom, she wasn't there. The smoke was so thick, they'd had no choice but to get themselves and their little boy to safety."

Gage's expression darkened and Megan knew that, as a parent, he could only imagine how it would feel to leave Ava behind in that situation.

"We found her," Megan said quickly. "She must have heard the neighbor pounding on the door and gotten scared. Small children tend to hide and she'd gone into the bedroom closet. She'd taken in some smoke but she was conscious.

"I handed her off to one of my partners and the next thing I knew, the floor caved in and I was falling. I woke up in the hospital forty-eight hours later and found out I'd gone straight to surgery. I had a mild concussion, but this arm—" she touched the scar "—and my leg took the brunt of the impact when I fell. I had a compound fracture of the radius and ended up with pins to hold it together."

There'd been two more surgeries to fix her knee.

"I was hopeful at first that I could go back to work…" Megan's voice trailed off. "But I would never want to be a liability to the department. It's a difficult job when you're in top physical condition but not if you're…weak."

"Weak?" Gage echoed. "Megan… I think you're incredibly strong."

The words warmed Megan's heart even though she knew he wouldn't be saying that if he'd seen her eight months ago.

"I was a wreck," she said candidly. "I'd poured so much into my career…into being the best…proving to everyone that I could do the job…that I didn't realize how much my life had gotten out of balance until everything fell apart.

"Those first few weeks, I was angry. I felt helpless. Alone."

She dared a look at Gage, just in time to see him

nod, as if there'd been a time in his life when he'd felt the same way.

"My grandma Lou told me that being a firefighter is what I did, it wasn't who I was." Megan smiled at the memory. *You are still a child of God. A daughter. A granddaughter. A sister. A friend. Those things haven't changed.*

"That's the day I started to ask God 'What should I do now?' instead of 'Why did this happen?' Then my best friend Jac stopped over. She works at a vet clinic, asked if I could foster a dog for a few weeks. He'd been traumatized and needed some time to heal." Megan smiled, remembering the morning Jac had shown up at her door. "I think she'd told Tux the same thing about me."

The Dalmatian's ears perked up at the sound of his name. While Baxter happily joined Ava in her antics, Tux remained close to Megan. Now he whined deep in his throat and propped his chin on her foot.

"I'd talked about taking in dogs 'someday,' but Tux made me realize that I could still dream."

"So you decided to start a rescue," Gage finished.

Megan nodded.

"I applied to teach a few first-responder classes through the technical college and I'll be starting in the fall," she told him. "Physically, I have some limitations now, but my grandma Lou said I have a lot up here—" she tapped her head "—to share."

Gage snorted softly. "It's nice to have a family member who believes in you. My dad calls once a week but it's only because he's still afraid that I'm going to run his business into the ground."

"I'm sure that's not true."

She'd had a glimpse at Gage's life when she'd read through his application. Did his dad not realize how hard he worked?

"Dad had high hopes for me," Gage said. "When I dropped out of college and came back to Pine Bridge with a newborn, it didn't exactly inspire confidence in my ability to make wise decisions."

So Gage had been trying to prove himself ever since?

"What happened to Ava's mom?" Megan asked cautiously.

"She decided she didn't want to be one." Gage's lips twisted. "I told Taylor we could make it work... become a family...but it turned out she didn't have much faith in me, either."

Without thinking, Megan reached for his hand. It was a gesture meant to comfort, but his fingers tangled with hers. Held on. And when she dared to look at Gage, she saw the heat of the campfire reflected in his eyes.

Gage leaned toward her. "Megan..."

"Look how many fireflies I caught!"

The lilting question broke the connection and Megan was suddenly free.

"How many?" Gage sounded so calm, Megan wondered if she'd imagined the last sixty seconds.

Had he really been about to kiss her? Or had she dreamt it?

Hoped for it?

Ava held out a glass Mason jar. "Fourteen," she said proudly.

Megan remained riveted to the chair as Gage rose to his feet.

"Time for you to let them go and for us to say good-night. It's a school day tomorrow."

Ava opened her mouth to protest but a yawn escaped instead.

"I'm not tired yet, Daddy."

Megan finally found her voice. "Baxter and Tux have to go to bed, too."

Baxter, who'd been searching the ground for stray bits of hot dog bun, looked up at the adults and heaved a sigh.

Megan chuckled. "Let's see if we can coax CB outside and take a quick walk first."

"I can do that while Ava helps you clean up," Gage suggested. "I won't say the password, but I still have some Cheetos in my pocket to use as a bribe."

He strode toward the house before Megan could respond. She began to stack the paper plates while Ava released the fireflies back into the grass and then collected the willow branches they'd used to roast the marshmallows.

"Miss Megan?"

"Mmm-hmm?" The porch light flipped on and Megan saw Gage and CB amble down the driveway.

The bribe must have worked.

"Do you want to go camping again?"

Megan smiled, charmed by the way Ava equated camping with having fun outdoors. "I'd love to."

"Really?" Ava's face lit up. "We can roast marshmallows. And paint our nails...and go exploring. And make a craft."

Paint their nails?

Megan had never considered manicures an outdoor activity but nail polish wouldn't be on Gage's list of things to purchase at the store.

"It sounds like fun."

Ava launched herself into Megan's arms. "I can't wait to tell Willow."

Willow, Megan recalled, was Ava's introverted friend who didn't like being called on during story time.

Gage returned with CB and scooped his daughter off the ground, set her on the ledge of his hip. "Say thank you to Megan for feeding us. Again."

"Thanks, Miss Megan."

"It's our turn next time," Gage said.

Next time.

Megan's heart warmed at the promise even as she told herself that Gage was only being a good neighbor.

And she, in the interest of being a good neighbor, too, would be happy to accept.

Chapter Eleven

"I'd just about given up on you, Lawrence. Don't you ever answer your phone?"

And hello to you, too.

Gage rolled down the passenger's-side window so CB could take in all the smells. He'd texted Megan on impulse after dropping Ava off at school and, with her permission, had stopped to pick up the Lab on his way to work. Gage hadn't even had to use the password to get CB out of his kennel. Megan had said the dog had heard his truck coming up the driveway and was standing at the door before he'd reached the house.

Anticipation.

Gage was guilty of the same thing.

He hadn't been able to stop thinking about Megan. Couldn't stop thinking about the warmth of her skin when she'd taken his hand. The way her lips had parted...

"Lawrence?"

Gage yanked his thoughts back in line.

"I'm sorry, Mr. Billings." He'd seen the three missed calls from Foster Billings on his phone but hadn't had an opportunity to return them. "I met with a potential client at a building site and there was no cell phone reception in the area."

"Your dad assured me that you were available

twenty-four-seven," Billings growled. "That's one of the reasons I was willing to sign a contract with you."

Was willing?

Gage recognized the word for what it was. A warning, not a slip of the tongue. A reminder that Foster could still change his mind and go in a different direction.

Not only was Billings an old friend of Gage's father's, he was a private developer who specialized in buying up land, making some improvements, and then dividing it into squares before selling it to people who wanted their own little piece of paradise.

A few months ago, Billings had driven through Pine Bridge, decided the town was a "diamond in the rough," and had reached out to Gage. Wanted to partner with him in a new venture—building the homes on spec once he found the perfect piece of property.

It was a partnership Gage couldn't afford to lose.

Billings had never worked with one builder while planning his developments. His decision to go with log-cabin-style vacation homes would not only give Triple L Builders more exposure than billboards and radio ads, it would guarantee a steady—and substantial—income for Gage's employees over the next few years.

Reasons he put up with Billings's somewhat abrasive personality.

"I'm sorry," he said again. Even while something inside of Gage knew it wasn't completely true.

Billings had left his first voice mail message when Gage had been reading a story to Ava after they'd returned from Megan's the night before. After tucking her in for the night, he'd realized how often his work days rolled into the evening hours.

How long had it been since he'd simply watched his daughter play? Soaked up the sound of her laughter? Taken a few moments to appreciate the stunning beauty of God's creation? Roasted marshmallows and counted fireflies?

Too long.

He and Ava were together a lot, but Gage realized the majority of their time was Ava joining Gage in his world. Driving to job sites or running errands. Sitting in the dugout while he coached or entertaining herself while he caught up on house and yardwork.

Gage had wanted to correct Ava when she'd told Megan they'd roasted marshmallows once, but when he'd searched his memory, that was all he could come up with, too.

Connie frequently told Gage that he should hire a site manager, but he hadn't gotten around to it yet, although there were several qualified candidates on his work crews. She'd even hinted that Gage was being a bit of a control freak, but every decision, good or bad, could affect his standing as a builder. He didn't want anything to slip through the cracks.

Especially his opportunity to build homes for Foster Billings, no matter how much of a pain in the neck the man could be.

"Time isn't just money, you know," Billings sputtered, not ready to let Gage off the hook yet. "It's a reflection of your priorities."

That's what Gage was afraid of.

"What can I do for you?" he asked before Billings could go on another rant.

"I have the paperwork ready to buy the perfect piece of land but there's a problem."

When it came to Billings, there always seemed to be a problem. But Gage had already spent countless hours drawing up a plan for five modest log homes. A last-minute glitch was the last thing he needed if something had finally caught the developer's eye.

"I didn't realize you were that close to making an offer," Gage said.

"That's because it wasn't for sale until my lawyer contacted the property owner last week and made one he couldn't refuse." Billings sounded smug. "But the clients who will purchase these homes are looking for peace and tranquility. A home away from home where they can enjoy nature. Put their feet up. The only noise they want to hear is the sound of birds singing while they drink their espresso on the deck."

"I haven't figured out a way to get birds to sing on cue," Gage joked.

Billings's silence told Gage he hadn't appreciated his attempt at levity.

"It's come to my attention that the person who recently bought the property next door could scare potential buyers away."

Gage buried a sigh. In a small town, these kinds of situations were tricky, but if he knew the parties involved, Gage supposed he could act as mediator.

"Where is the property you're interested in purchasing?"

"Fifteen acres on Townline Road."

Gage lived on Townline Road. And there was only one parcel with that much acreage that would lend itself to the development Billings had envisioned.

Right next to Megan's.

"What do you mean 'scare potential buyers away'?" Gage asked cautiously.

"Dogs," was the blunt response. "Some woman with a bleeding heart is starting a shelter and no one is going to want their espresso time disrupted by barking and howling. Or worse, dogs running loose around the neighborhood."

Gage's breath stalled in his lungs. He thought about Megan's vision. How she wanted people to see Homeward Bound as part of the community. "It's not a shelter, Mr. Billings. It's a rescue."

"What's the difference?" Billings snarled. "The property value will go down the minute those kennels go up."

"I'm not sure you can do anything at this point, Mr. Billings," Gage said truthfully. "Megan Albright has the freedom to operate a dog rescue on her property."

"No, she doesn't." Billings sounded smug again. "I did a little digging and it turns out a portion of that road is on city water and sewer. My lawyer found an ordinance that a property owner who resides within the city limits can only have two dogs on the premises without special permission from the city council."

Gage had no knowledge of the ordinance, which meant it was so old that everyone had forgotten about it.

"You don't know the dogs will be a nuisance," he said. "The ordinance can be waived based on the circumstances. Megan has already invested—" *everything* "—her time and resources into the rescue and plans to open the end of next month. I'm sure she'll appeal and ask for a waiver."

"I hope she does because that's where you come in. Deny her request. And if the members aren't sure what to do, help them make up their minds."

Gage's gut clenched.

"Given the circumstances, some people might think that's a conflict of interest," he pointed out quietly.

"I think five new homes means that you look out for *my* interests," Billings shot back. "Otherwise, I might be forced to look for property somewhere else."

Billings didn't have to say the words out loud. His meaning was clear.

He'd find another builder, too.

Megan left the hardware store with a gallon of Winter Solstice paint, a package of brushes, and a craving for something sweet.

It seemed providential that The Three Chocolatiers was right across the street.

The few times Megan had ventured into town after moving to Pine Bridge, her destination had been the hardware store, where she'd stared at displays filled with paint chips instead of the mouth-watering array of homemade candy that she could see through the window of the confectionary shop.

Maybe she could buy something for Gage as a thank you.

A smile curved Megan's lips as she crossed the street.

A few hours after he'd spirited CB off for the day, another truck had pulled into her driveway. The man who'd hopped down from the cab had tipped his ball cap politely, introduced himself as Wayne, informed her that he was a plumber, and did Megan have time to show him where she wanted the washing station to go?

Megan, who'd planned to run errands, had made the time. And when she'd left, he was hard at work, whistling to a country song while another one of Megan's visions became a reality.

Thanks to Gage.

Bells jingled over the door as Megan stepped inside.

The interior was as charming as the brick storefront, with a tiled floor and a chalkboard wall advertising the daily specials. A granite countertop lined with vinyl stools ran the length of the room and bistro-style tables and chairs encouraged people to linger a while.

A woman wearing an apron over her daffodil-yellow sundress appeared from behind a gingham curtain. Megan recognized her instantly. She was the one who'd been talking to Gage after church service.

"Good morning!" The smile she cast in Megan's direction was friendly. And a little curious. Clover-green eyes traveled over Megan's lightweight sweater and faded jeans. Paused for a moment on the gallon of paint clutched in Megan's hand. "Today we're giving out samples of our strawberry shortcake and lemon meringue truffles, if you'd like to try one. Or both."

In spite of the fact that Megan felt frumpy and awkward compared to the perky woman behind the counter, she found herself returning her smile. "Both."

"Good choice." The woman glided over to a silver platter near the cash register. She grabbed the tongs and deposited two pieces of candy that looked like miniature works of art on a paper plate.

"Is this your shop?" Megan asked.

"It's a family business. My aunt and uncle took it over from my grandparents years ago, but Aunt Hope is alone now so I've been helping out. I'm Delaney Anderson, by the way."

"It's nice to meet you. I'm—"

"Miss Megan!"

A door near the back of the shop swung open and two small figures rushed in.

Suddenly, Ava's arms were around her and she found herself on the receiving end of an exuberant hug.

"Well, hello there." Megan hugged her back. "I didn't expect to see you here."

The look of surprise on Delaney Anderson's face changed to speculation and Megan wondered what the woman was thinking.

Ava giggled. "I'm playing with Willow 'cause Daddy's working late again."

Willow. Ava's best friend.

And it seemed the girls' parents were close, too, if Gage called on Delaney for backup.

"A piece of equipment broke down and Gage asked if I'd keep an eye on Ava until he got back," Delaney explained. "My shift usually ends when school gets out, but my aunt is running late at a doctor appointment. I gave the girls a snack and they've been playing in the fenced-in patio out back."

"We're not playing, Mama," Willow said. "We're camping."

Delaney's lips twitched. "Sorry. My mistake."

"Come see!" Ava tugged on Megan's arm.

Megan glanced at Delaney and the woman nodded. "I have to check on something in the kitchen anyway."

The girls led the way to an adorable flagstone patio decorated with strings of lights and faux ferns in colorful ceramic pots.

"We made a tent." Ava pointed to a tablecloth draped over two bistro chairs.

Willow smiled shyly at Megan as she peeled back a corner of the cloth. "Want to look inside?"

Megan knelt and peeked through the gap. They'd created a table from a woven placemat, which held the remains of the snack Delaney had provided.

"Sorry. That took longer than I'd expected." Willow's mom had returned. "I'm discovering that chocolate is a little like clay and can be fussy to work with."

"That's all right." Megan rose and realized her knee didn't protest as much as it usually did. "The girls gave me a tour of their tent."

"Can't you stay a little longer?" Willow asked.

"We're going to roast marshmallows like you and Ava and Mr. Gage did."

Delaney's eyes widened and Megan felt a slow burn in her cheeks. "Baxter and Tux will be anxious for their walk."

"Wait!" Ava grabbed her backpack and started rummaging through it. "Don't forget your inbitation."

Inbitation?

Megan understood when Ava pulled out a piece of paper and handed it to her.

"It's for the campout," Willow said. "We're going to make crafts and sing songs and stuff."

Megan tried not to let her confusion show. When Ava had asked her if she wanted to go camping, she hadn't realized Willow would be "inbited," too.

Or that there would be an official date.

That, according to the information written in pink marker, was only two weeks away.

"Willow…where did that invitation come from?" Delaney's voice sounded a little strained.

"We copied mine," the little girl said cheerfully. "Johanna's mom didn't have any more."

Okay. Now Megan was really confused. She didn't know Johanna or her mom, but it occurred to her that she should have asked Ava more questions before she'd agreed to go camping again.

"Girls…why don't you play for a few minutes while I box up Miss Megan's order?" Delaney said.

They disappeared inside the tent and Megan followed Delaney back into the store.

"Ava asked me if I wanted to go camping again, but

I thought she meant at my house, with hot dogs and marshmallows," Megan said once they were inside. "But this—" she held up the card "—looks more official. Is the school or church sponsoring it?"

"Not exactly." Delaney bit her lip but Megan couldn't tell if it was because the situation was getting awkward or she was trying not to laugh. "Miranda Waverly, Johanna's mom, is hosting a Glampout for some of her friends in their class."

Oh. Megan winced.

"I had no idea. I didn't mean to intrude if you and Gage decided that you would take both the girls."

"I planned to take Willow. And there is no me and Gage," Delaney added, so firmly that Megan believed her. She paused for a moment, as if wondering how much to say. "The campout is for mothers and daughters."

Megan's gaze dropped to the date on the invitation and realized it lined up with Mother's Day weekend.

"I already told her I'd go." Megan groaned. "Why would Ava invite me to this? I'm not a mom."

Delaney did smile now. "Maybe she's hoping that changes."

Chapter Twelve

Maybe she's hoping that changes.

Delaney's words continued to cycle through Megan's mind on the drive home.

How had she gotten herself into such a predicament?

She'd have to find a way to get out of the commitment without disappointing the little girl who, in such a short time, had worked her way into Megan's heart.

Along with her father.

Megan didn't even try to shush the teasing inner voice this time.

It was true.

She didn't know what to do about that, either.

Megan was tempted to call Jac, but her friend would love to say "I told you so" and Megan didn't know if she was ready to put a name to the feelings she had for Gage.

What Megan *did* know was that she'd have to talk to him about Ava's invitation.

How would Gage react when he found out his daughter was playing matchmaker?

Megan stopped at the mailbox and made a mental note to get a new one when rust sprinkled down like confetti as she pried open the door.

Other than junk mail addressed to the previous owner, Megan hadn't received anything since she'd moved in, but today there was a letter with Megan's name on it.

A silly thing but her heart lifted a little. One more small affirmation that she belonged here. She tucked it into the pocket of her denim jacket and drove up to the house.

She parked the car in front of the garage. Wayne had left for the day but the curtains moved in the window, propelled by Baxter's wagging tail. Megan was anxious to see the progress on the washing station but she took a minute to let the dogs out first.

Baxter launched off the porch like a furry cannonball while Tux gave Megan his accusing why-did-you-leave-me stare before he attached himself to her side.

"I know neither one of you is wild about baths, but I'm going to need a volunteer to test this out when it's done," Megan warned them.

She opened the door and stepped inside the shed. It took a moment for Megan to realize that the washing station wasn't a work in progress. She'd only been gone several hours but it was finished. New drain tile. A gleaming faucet and hand-held shower. There was even a fancy shampoo and soap dispenser mounted on the wall.

Baxter and Tux were more interested in the left-overs from the lunch the plumber had tossed into the trash, but Megan was blown away. All she had to do was add a bench and shelving with cubbies to hold supplies, and they were open for business.

"This calls for a celebration," she told the dogs. "But we have to wait for CB."

That meant waiting for Gage.

She bent down to pick up a stray bolt that Wayne had missed during cleanup. The envelope slipped from her pocket and drifted to the floor.

Megan looked at the return address for the first time and frowned. The name of the law firm wasn't familiar but it wasn't the first time she'd received a letter from a personal injury attorney hoping to lay the blame—and financial burden—on someone for her accident.

She opened it and a cold hand gripped her heart as she skimmed through the opening paragraph.

Dear Ms. Albright,
It has come to our attention...

The words blurred as Megan read it again. And again.

The rumble of an engine outside barely registered until she heard a door slam, followed by a familiar voice.

"Come on, CB. We missed your curfew, so no lagging. Megan is probably wondering if I dognapped you."

Megan stumbled out of the shed. Both her knees felt wobbly. Weak.

"There you..." The smile on Gage's face disappeared. "What's wrong?"

Megan held up the letter. "This came in the mail today. It's from an attorney, letting me know that if

I open the rescue, I'll be violating a city ordinance against having more than two dogs on my property.

"They sent it on behalf of their client, but I have no idea what Billings Development Company is...or does."

Megan suddenly realized that although Gage's expression had darkened, he didn't look shocked by the news.

He nodded curtly. "The ordinance was put into place years ago when someone got caught running a puppy mill."

"But... I don't understand. Why would they be sending me a letter?"

Gage raked his hand through his hair. "Billings specializes in purchasing land he thinks will appeal to people looking for a second home away from home. He's concerned that potential buyers will be turned off when they find out there's a dog rescue so close to their luxury vacation homes."

"That's ridiculous," Megan protested. "Why would he target me? I'm nowhere near his property."

"You will be. The vacant land he wants to put an offer on is right next to yours."

Gage wasn't looking at her now. His gaze was fixed on the thick hedge of trees behind her.

"You knew about this, didn't you?" Megan could hardly breathe.

"Megan—"

"Didn't you?"

"Yes." The word rolled out with a sigh. "But I didn't

know he'd be sending you a letter. Billings contacted me this morning about the ordinance."

"Of course." Megan couldn't prevent the bitterness from leaking into her voice. "He wants the chairman of the city council on his side. You know the rescue won't be a problem. What kind of recourse do I have? I can't afford an attorney to fight this. Can I meet with the city council and appeal my case?"

Megan paused to take a breath, waiting for him to tell her that everything would work out. That her dream wasn't in jeopardy.

He didn't.

And then Megan understood.

"You're building the houses for him."

"Yes, but I might be able to convince Billings to drop it."

Might?

The word drummed in Megan's head.

"And if you can't?"

"I don't know." The slight edge in Gage's voice cut deep. "But this is a big contract, Megan. I need some time to think about it."

"Don't let me get in the way. Not that I would."

"What is that supposed to mean?"

"Never mind." Megan pivoted away from him and almost tripped over Tux.

Gage reached out to steady her and she pulled away. "Please, just go."

Megan could feel Gage watching her as she walked up the driveway, yet he didn't call her name. Ask her to come back so they could talk about it.

Gage wanted his business to be a success. Partnering with Billings would give him more than capital. It would boost his reach and his reputation as a builder. Prove to his dad once and for all that he was a success.

Gage claimed he needed time to think about it, but his silence proved he'd already made his decision.

"Your attorney sent a letter to Megan Albright."

Gage's back teeth slammed together when he heard Billings chuckle on the other end of the line.

"I told you the first time we met that I get things done."

"There's a right way to go about it, though." Gage struggled to stay calm but all he could see was the stricken look on Megan's face before she'd left him standing in the driveway.

And like an idiot, he'd let her go.

"This is the right way. Pine Bridge came up with the ordinance, not me," Billings retorted, not the least bit concerned that he had the power to crush Megan's dream.

Because he expected Gage to do it for him.

"I've already got three interested buyers," Billings said. "By the time we break ground, I guarantee every lot will be sold."

We.

Until today, partnering with the developer had triggered a sense of pride. Accomplishment. Now Gage felt...trapped.

"Megan Albright purchased her property because

she thought it would be the perfect place for the rescue," he said slowly.

"Maybe she'll decide to relocate," Billings said jovi-
ally. "I'll buy her land and we can put a few houses on
it, too. Your dad said you get things done, too, Gage.
This is your chance to prove it."

He ended the call before Gage could comment.

Not that he could have. The thought of Megan selling her home, leaving Pine Bridge, made it impossible
for Gage to think let alone speak.

He pulled into a parking space in front of The Three
Chocolatiers and waited for his blood pressure to go
down before he went inside to get Ava.

He spotted Delaney behind the counter and her
careful smile told Gage that something unexpected
must have upended her day. Her aunt Hope typically
worked the afternoon shift so Delaney could pick up
Willow after school.

"Sorry I'm late." Gage said the words automati-
cally and then realized he'd been saying them way
too much lately.

Ever since he'd taken over the business, Gage had
been making apologies and excuses. To other people.
To Ava.

To himself.

*That's the day I started to ask God "What should I
do now?" instead of "Why did this happen?"* Megan
had told him.

Gage realized he hadn't been asking for guidance
at all. Oh, he talked the talk. Nodded when the pas-

tor preached about God being in control while setting his own course.

And then Megan confessed she'd done the same thing and made Gage examine his priorities. And his motives.

"The girls are playing on the patio—" Delaney stopped as the door swung open and Ava and Willow charged in. "I take it back. They're right here."

"Thanks again, Delaney." Gage grabbed Ava's backpack and took her hand. "I owe you."

"I'll remind you of that on every major holiday." Delaney smiled. "We need the business."

"Where's CB?" Ava asked the moment she spotted the empty passenger seat.

"I already dropped him off at Miss Megan's."

"I wanted to tell her that she's supposed to bring her own sleeping bag and pillow."

Gage tried to pull his thoughts back together. "Bring them where?"

"To the campout."

On top of everything else that had happened that day, Gage really didn't want to deal with this. A stabbing pain sank its talons into the base of his skull and settled there.

"Megan can't go to the campout because it's for mothers and daughters, Ava," he explained gently. "And that's why you didn't get an invitation—"

"I did, too!" Ava interrupted. "Johanna said it was okay. And me and Willow gave Miss Megan an inbitation when she was at the candy store today. She promised she'd come."

Maybe she had. But Gage doubted Megan had been given all the details.

"I know Megan is special to you, sweetheart, but in order to be your mom, she and I would have to be married."

"I know," Ava said matter-of-factly. "But I like Miss Megan. She's nice and fun, and I think she likes us, too."

"I'm afraid it isn't as simple as that."

Especially now that Gage was the obstacle standing between Megan and her dream.

Chapter Thirteen

"Not today, buddy. I'm sorry."

CB, who'd come out of his kennel after breakfast without any coaxing from Megan and padded over to the window, didn't take his gaze off the driveway.

"I can take you for a ride." Although Megan's compact might not be an adequate substitute for Gage's pickup.

CB flopped down on the rug in front of the window, as if he wasn't ready to give up hope yet.

Megan wished she could be more like the Lab.

Her cell began to ring and she saw Jac's number appear on the screen. Ignoring it would only delay the inevitable, so she answered with a cheerful good morning, thankful that Jac couldn't see the dark circles under her eyes.

"I'm on my way to work but I had to give you a quick call," Jac said. "Do you remember the dogs I mentioned last week? The ones the deputies brought into the vet?"

"Uh-huh." Megan cut a piece of the coffee cake she'd baked at 4:00 a.m. and slid it onto a plate.

"We're looking for a foster home for two of them. They're bonded siblings, so they can share a kennel," Jac continued. "I figured with the rate things are moving along at your place, you might have some space available soon."

Megan's throat tightened.

Things weren't moving along. Things had come to a dead standstill.

With the rescue and her relationship with Gage.

That wasn't a relationship, Megan reminded herself sternly. She wasn't sure what it was, but she'd been dreaming about what it *could* be and that's what hurt the most when he'd watched her walk away.

"I'm sorry, Jac. I… I can't."

"What happened?" Jac immediately picked up on the faint wobble in Megan's voice. "The last time we talked, it sounded like you'd be opening ahead of schedule."

Megan poured out the whole story, telling her about Gage's partnership with the developer who thought a rescue would ruin his plans for the property, and about Ava's invitation to the upcoming Glampout.

"I didn't know it was an organized event—"

"Whoa. Back up." Jac demanded. "Gage's daughter invited you to a mother-daughter campout?"

"Uh-huh. I thought we were going to recreate our campfire and marshmallow night, so I said yes."

"You had a campfire and marshmallows? Was Gage there, too?"

"He was bringing CB back and I had a fire going… more hotdogs than I could eat…"

"Why did Gage have CB?"

"He figured out that CB likes trucks."

Too late, Megan realized she should have spelled the word. CB's tail began to wag and he looked out the window again.

Jac lapsed into silence for a moment but Megan could practically hear the hum of the wheels turning in her friend's head.

"So, you'll go to the city council meeting and state your case. It's not like you're going *One Hundred and One Dalmatians* on them. You're only taking in a few dogs at a time, and I'm sure some people on the board have fur babies and will appreciate what you're doing. You could round up support. Maybe Gage would write a letter on your behalf."

"He's the council chair."

"And you didn't lead with that?" The question was punctuated by something that sounded a lot like a hand smacking a forehead. "That's great! Gage has been helping you get the rescue ready. He understands your vision, right?"

Yes, but Gage had a vision, too.

"Did you miss the part about Gage working with Billings? He'll side with him and the rescue...well, we might have to face the fact it isn't going to happen."

"No, we aren't. You're going to call Grandma Lou and we're all going to pray," Jac said. "Just like we did when you were recovering from the accident. God was with you then and He isn't going to abandon you now."

"You're right. But—"

"No buts. And you're going to the Glampout with Ava, too. I'll come over and watch the dogs for the weekend."

"I have a counterfeit invitation written in pink marker," Megan pointed out. "I'm not sure they'll let me in."

"You've run into burning buildings," Jac said. "Compared with that, this will be a piece of cake."

"It's a mom-and-daughter thing. I'm just the next-door neighbor."

"You must be more than that to Ava. She wants you there, Megs. And I think you want to be there, too."

Jac was right. But then, she usually was.

That was why, the moment after they said goodbye, Megan took a deep breath and called Grandma Lou.

"Why can't I go to Miss Megan's house?"

Because Gage hadn't seen or spoken to her for a week. And because Megan wouldn't be at home. She would be attending the city council meeting.

"Willow is expecting you," Gage said instead. "She'd be disappointed if you didn't come over."

"I guess." Ava dragged the toe of her sandal across the floor. "But I miss Baxter. Can we go over there tomorrow?"

"You're going with me to baseball practice, remember?"

Ava's response was a drawn-out sigh before she retreated to the family room to play. Leaving Gage alone with nothing but his guilty conscience for company.

He'd been dodging Ava's frequent requests to visit Megan just like he'd been dodging phone calls from his dad.

As if on cue, his cell began to ring.

Gage considered ignoring it, but his dad might show up at the door if he let it go to voice mail again.

"Hey, Dad. I'm almost ready to walk out the door—"

"Hey to you, too. And I know. I wanted to catch you before the meeting tonight."

Gage wasn't surprised Billings had been in touch with his father.

"If you're worried that I'm going to lose the contract—"

"I'm worried about you," his dad interrupted. "When I spoke with Foster, he seemed to think you have a problem with enforcing the ordinance."

"Because I don't believe people will be reluctant to buy lots next door to the rescue. There's a quarter acre of trees acting as a buffer between Megan's property and the new development," Gage told him. "She has two dogs of her own and doesn't plan to take in more rescues than she can handle. Homeward Bound isn't some fly-by-night operation, Dad. Megan has thought everything through and she wants to partner with the community."

"Is that why you pulled a roofing crew and one of your plumbers off the job and sent them over there?"

"Are you *spying* on me?"

"Please. I don't need satellites or drones. I talk to my six-year-old granddaughter every week and she knows everything that goes on. It sounds to me like she's quite attached to this Megan," he mused. "And I was wondering if maybe my son is, too."

His dad never asked about his personal life. He talked about business. The weather. The price of fuel.

Gage was so stunned, it didn't occur to him to avoid the topic.

"It won't matter after tonight, will it?"

"I guess that's up to you."

"Wait. What? Are you saying that I should side with Megan? Billings already threatened to pull out of the deal if I didn't convince the rest of the board to uphold the ordinance."

"Foster Billings would be making a mistake," his dad said quietly. "I don't want you to make a bigger one."

"But you always put the company first."

Silence stretched between them. "After your mom left us, I threw myself into work," his dad finally said. "I always wanted to travel, but set it aside for 'someday.' And then I met Diana and realized I wanted to enjoy today. With her.

"I wanted you to follow in my footsteps and run the family business, but I don't want you to make the same mistake I did and put business before family. I can attest to how quickly kids grow up. Don't let these years with Ava slip away. And, Gage…losing a deal doesn't compare to losing someone you care about."

Gage realized he wasn't talking about Ava now.

"Billings has a lot of connections. If I back out, it could hurt Triple L's reputation."

Instead of agreeing, his dad actually chuckled.

"*You're* Triple L Builders, Gage. People want you to build their home because they trust you. You care about the process from start to finish. No one, not even Billings, can take that away from you."

Gage's watch beeped a reminder, jolting him out of his state of shock.

"Dad... I have to go or I'll be late."

"Whatever you decide...you know I'm proud of you."

His dad's words echoed inside of Gage's head as he hurried Ava out the door and dropped her off at Delaney's apartment.

He knew there'd been talk when he'd returned to Pine Bridge as a single dad, so he'd poured himself into the business. Tried to convince himself the sacrifices he made were for Ava's future. The good of the community. A man's reputation was important, so Gage had done everything he could to protect it.

But it suddenly occurred to Gage there was something else he'd been trying to protect.

His heart.

And by trying to avoid being hurt, he'd hurt the woman he was falling for.

No. *Had* fallen for.

His dad said people trusted him, but would Megan?

Billings met him in the foyer of the community center, where the council held their monthly meetings.

"Fate has smiled on us, Lawrence." The developer grinned. "That Albright woman won't be attending the meeting after all. She claimed she had a family emergency."

Gage's heart slammed against his rib cage. "What kind of emergency?"

"I have no idea." Billings shrugged. "But now she

can't share her sob story about abandoned dogs and convince the council to vote in her favor."

Losing a deal doesn't compare to losing someone you care about.

Gage grinned back.

"It doesn't matter if Megan is here to state her case or not," he said. "Because I will."

Chapter Fourteen

"Thank you, Megan." Miranda Waverly, Johanna's mom, accepted a plate with a stack of pancakes. "These look delicious. I'm afraid my cooking skills are limited to what I can make in the microwave oven."

"The fire department held a breakfast fundraiser every year and I was in charge of the griddle."

The woman standing behind Miranda in the breakfast line clucked her tongue and leaned closer to Megan. "Miranda's on the fundraising committee for the elementary school. Be careful what you say."

Megan laughed. "I'll remember that."

Any fear about showing up at the campground on Saturday, an hour late and with a handwritten invitation, had been put to rest by the warm welcome Megan had received from Johanna's mom and the rest of the women. Almost as if they'd been expecting her.

That had been a relief, because she'd never crashed a party before.

Then again, she'd never been sweetly but firmly kicked out of her grandma Lou's house, either, but that had happened, too.

When she'd called her grandma to ask for prayer, she'd sounded tired, not at all like herself. Megan had planned to check in on her later in the day, but a few hours later, she'd received a call from the hospital. Megan had packed a bag, supplies for the dogs, and left for Eau Claire. She wasn't sure how long she'd be staying, but once Grandma Lou was settled in at home again, she'd made the decision for her.

I appreciate you being here for me, but I'll be fine. And a little bird told me that you have special plans for the weekend.

A little bird? More like a stool pigeon.

Jac, who loved Grandma Lou just as much as Megan, had stopped by for a visit and must have spilled the beans.

There'd been a smile on her grandmother's face and a twinkle in her eye when she'd told Megan to pack her bag, leaving Megan to wonder what else Jac had said about the Lawrence family.

Then there'd been the text from Delaney Anderson, telling Megan that she and Willow would be picking up Ava on their way to the campground, but they'd save a bunk in their cabin for her.

If Megan didn't know better, she'd think it was a conspiracy.

Megan had repacked her bag and driven back to Pine Bridge with Grandma Lou's blessing. And a promise from Jac that she would be at Megan's house by suppertime with the dogs so Megan could go straight to the campground.

The afternoon was sunny and warm, perfect for outdoor activities. She and Ava had gone hiking, taken part in a scavenger hunt and painted their nails. After supper, there was a sing-along around the campfire and s'mores. When she'd finally fallen into her bunk,

Megan had found a note and the bracelet Ava had woven out of embroidery floss during craft time.

Mis Megen Thank you for being my mom for the day. Lov Ava

Megan had felt tears sting the backs of her eyes when she'd slipped the bracelet on her wrist.

Ava needed a mom who would be there *every* day, to giggle with, to kiss away the hurts.

But it wouldn't be her.

Gage didn't have room in his life for love. It was all about his career.

"Miss Megan! Can I have a pancake, too?"

The question yanked Megan back to the present. She filled a plate for Willow and grabbed another one for Delaney.

"I don't know about you, but I like this kind of camping." Delaney sighed. "I say we do this every Mother's Day."

Megan forced a smile. She could see a friendship blossoming between her and Willow's mom, but wasn't sure if she would be in Pine Bridge a year from now.

"One pancake or two?" Megan's gaze shifted to Ava, who was standing behind Willow in the line.

Ava shrugged. "I'm not hungry," she mumbled.

"You need your energy for the hike up to the waterfall this morning," Megan said.

"Is it going to take a long time?"

Megan tried to mask her surprise, knowing how much Ava loved to explore. "No, but we'll be having a picnic lunch there. And I think I heard Johanna's mom mention a special guest."

"Oh." Ava nibbled on her lower lip. "Can we go now?"

It took a moment for Megan to realize she wasn't talking about the hike. "You want to go home? Aren't you feeling well?"

"I'm okay."

The fact she wouldn't make eye contact with Megan said otherwise.

Megan wasn't sure about the protocol for leaving early, but she didn't want to force Ava to stay if she was coming down with something. She sought out Miranda and thanked her, told Delaney she would be dropping Ava off at home, and packed up their camping gear.

Ava was quiet for several miles, but when they turned onto Townline Road, she leaned forward.

"Can I say hi to Baxter?"

Megan glanced in the rearview mirror. Ava had perked up, her hazel eyes as bright as her smile again.

Megan hesitated. If there was something wrong, she wasn't sure a detour was a good idea. But then, she wasn't in a big hurry to see Gage.

He'd left a message the night of the city council meeting, asking Megan to call him back, but Grandma Lou had been transferred to the ICU with a high fever and severe dehydration within hours of Megan's arrival, so she hadn't been able to.

She had no idea what the council members had decided, but Megan had been too tired and worried to think about the future of the rescue. To think about her last conversation with Gage, either.

He might feel bad for her, but how could he pass up a partnership with a developer who would help him achieve his goals?

"Please? Just for a few minutes?" Ava pleaded. "I think he misses me."

"All right." Megan gave in. "Just a few minutes."

She knew Jac would love to meet Ava before she went home.

Megan rounded the corner at the end of the driveway, but in front of the house, where her friend's car should have been parked, was a familiar silver pickup truck.

Gage hadn't been this nervous since he'd changed a diaper for the first time.

The campout officially ended at three o'clock, but the crunch of tires on the driveway snagged Gage's attention and he looked out the window.

They were early.

Jac had cheerfully taken Gage up on his offer to relieve her of dog-sitting duty when he'd shown up, but Ava must have been anxious to show Megan the changes that had been made in her absence and come up with an excuse to leave early.

And now Gage was part of the surprise.

Tux and Baxter heard the slam of the car door and streaked ahead of him.

Megan bent down to greet the dogs but her gaze remained locked on Gage, her expression guarded. Another sign he'd damaged her trust.

"Hi, Daddy!" Ava made a beeline for Gage the moment her feet hit the ground. "We had so much fun!"

Gage swept her into his arms. "I knew you would."

"Can we show Miss Megan now?" she said in a loud whisper.

"Sure," Gage whispered back.

Ava wiggled free and grabbed Megan's hand. "Come on!"

Megan cast a confused look at Gage but followed her into the building. Pulled up short.

"The kennels." She stared at the three indoor runs. "You finished them."

"With a little help," Gage said. "It wasn't free, though. You're on the hook for another batch of chocolate-chip cookies."

Megan opened the kennel door, looked down at the thick rubber mat that lined the floor.

"Ron said you wanted to go with this instead of concrete."

Megan dipped her chin in a nod but didn't say anything.

Why wasn't she saying anything?

Gage was starting to doubt the "let's surprise Megan" strategy.

Ava, who'd been cuddling Baxter, turned a circle in the center of the room. "Where's CB?"

"Napping in his kennel," Gage said. He saw Megan's expression and frowned. "Isn't he?"

"He was only here for a short visit," she said. "I had to bring all three dogs with me when I heard Grandma

Lou was in the hospital. Jac decided he was doing a lot better, so she took him back to the shelter."

"Will he be okay?" Ava looked worried.

"Jac will keep a close eye on him," Megan promised. "And she'll help him find a forever family."

Ava looked uncertain and looped her arms around Baxter's neck as if she were afraid he might disappear, too.

"Aves," Gage said gently. "I'm sure Baxter would love to play tag with you."

Ava looked at Megan and she nodded. Added the smile he'd been hoping to see since she'd arrived.

"Come on, boys!" Ava patted her leg and darted out the door.

To Gage's surprise, both dogs followed her outside.

Megan bent down and pushed on the flap of the dog door. On the other side was the fenced-in run sandwiched between the two kennels Gage had finished the day before.

She straightened, twisted to face him. "I don't understand. Why would you do all this? Your voice mail said the council would review the ordinance and make a decision at the next meeting."

So, she *had* listened to it. Megan hadn't called him back so Gage hadn't been sure.

"The council hasn't made a decision yet, but I did," he said. "I told Billings that if he was against the rescue, he'd have to look for another piece of land to develop."

"But…" Confusion darkened Megan's eyes. "What about the houses? You'll lose all that income."

"Triple L will be okay. I realized he wasn't the kind of partner I wanted to work with anyway. There will be other opportunities."

Instead of throwing her arms around him—Gage had been kind of looking forward to that—Megan took a step away from him.

Okay. She needed some more convincing.

"I realized something else." And Gage hoped it wasn't too late. "I would rather make time for the people I care about than make another deal. I don't want to have regrets, like my dad. We might not get a do-over, but it's never too late to *start* over."

Tears shimmered in Megan's eyes and Gage drew in a breath, reached into the back pocket of his jeans.

"And in case you don't believe me, here's the proof."

"What's this?"

Megan stared down at the envelope in his hand.

Gage had the audacity to wink—*wink*—at Megan as he opened the flap and removed a sheaf of papers. "I updated my application."

Application?

Megan tried to focus on the envelope, but her mind was replaying what Gage had just said.

I would rather make time for the people I care about.

Was he talking about her?

Hope welled up inside Megan even though a part of her was afraid to believe it was true.

"Gage…that wasn't necessary."

"Yes, it was. Take a look at the references. Page five," he added helpfully.

Megan knew where it was and battled a strong urge to smile.

"You added my grandma Lou? And Jac?"

"Connie found their addresses and we've been texting." Gage looked pleased with himself. "You'll notice some changes under the lifestyle section, too."

Megan tried to concentrate on the words but it was impossible when Gage was standing so close. "I don't—"

"No more coaching baseball," Gage said. "And after my term is up next month, I'm stepping down from the city council. I also hired Ryan to be my site manager and troubleshooter so my work day won't spill out into the evenings and weekends."

Megan swallowed hard. "Ava will be happy."

"I know what would make her happier."

Megan did smile now. "A puppy?"

"Spending more time with you."

"I'd like that, too," Megan murmured.

"We're kind of a package deal, though. I realize I'm not perfect," he added quickly. "Connie tells me that I'm stubborn. And I am a get-it-done instead of stop-and-smell-the-roses kind of guy. But I'm trying. So, if you can put up with me…"

The words were teasing but Megan heard the hint of uncertainty in Gage's voice and knew it was her turn to take a risk.

Because Gage was patient. Funny. A loving dad. A good neighbor. A man who'd ridden to her rescue in a silver pickup truck even when she hadn't needed rescuing.

The kind of man she'd dreamed about.

"I'm looking forward to it," Megan said honestly.

Gage unleashed a slow smile.

"And I've been looking forward to this." He drew Megan slowly into the circle of his arms and captured her lips.

The kiss was like Gage, tender and passionate, and Megan tasted the sweetness of moments like this. A healing from the past and the promise of a future together.

When they finally broke apart, both of them were out of breath.

"Do you have any other plans for the day?" Gage's arms tightened around her.

"No." Megan was content to stay right there.

"Feel like taking a road trip?"

She tipped her head to look at him. "A road trip? Where?"

Gage smiled again. "To get CB."

"You want to adopt him?"

"You said he needed a forever family. Why not start today? And I am approved, right?"

Megan laughed. "Yes. You're approved."

Gage bent his head and kissed her again.

Love welled up inside Megan and another dream, one she hadn't dared to give a voice to, suddenly seemed within reach.

Because Gage was right.

This was a good day to start forever.

Epilogue

Four Months Later

"Hurry up, Daddy! I don't want to be late!"

"I'm right behind—" *You.*

The screen door snapped shut before Gage could finish the sentence.

Okay. He was a little excited, too. And nervous.

Gage stepped outside. Ava was already in the truck and CB had commandeered his usual spot in the front passenger seat.

"Do you think Daisy will like me?" Ava asked as they started down the road.

"Megan said she's very friendly."

"What kind of dog is she?"

"I'm not sure." Gage hedged. "She wants it to be a surprise."

"I like surprises."

Gage hoped Megan did, too.

Lately, the mile-long drive to her house felt like a hundred. It was getting more and more difficult to say goodbye to her at the end of the day.

When they arrived, Megan was standing outside the kennel at the end of the driveway, cradling a wiggling ball of golden fluff in her arms.

"A puppy!" Ava squealed.

Gage had been too busy staring at Megan to notice.

Today she wore slim-fitting jeans and a sweatshirt with the Homeward Bound Rescue logo silkscreened on the front that she teasingly referred to as "free advertising." Not that she needed it. Word of mouth continued to spread around the community and she'd already found homes for six dogs since the rescue's official opening that spring.

Ava bailed from the back seat as soon as Gage parked the truck and scampered over to greet the new arrival. Megan carefully transferred the puppy into his daughter's arms, coaching her on the proper way to hold it. Ava listened intently and, once again, Gage silently thanked God for bringing Megan into their lives.

Over the course of the summer, she'd baked cookies with Ava and taught Gage the secret to making braids that were straight instead of crooked. They'd had countless campfires in the evenings. Laughed more. Counted fireflies and stars.

Megan might not be Ava's mom but she had a mother's heart. And she'd brought Gage's back to life again.

"So, what do you think of Daisy?" Megan asked when Ava set the puppy carefully on the ground.

"She's so sweet." Ava extracted a wrinkled piece of paper from the pocket of her jeans. "I have a list of people who might want to 'dopt her."

"Another list?" Gage teased.

Megan was working hard to suppress a smile as she skimmed through the names. "Willow?"

Ava bobbed her head. "Dogs don't make her sneeze, only cats."

"That's good to know," Megan said solemnly. "But

Willow and Miss Delaney live with their aunt and they don't have a lot of extra space for a dog."

"Daisy is little." Ava wasn't ready to cross out the Anderson family.

"I have an idea." Gage gave his daughter's braid a tug. "Why don't you take Daisy to the play yard? It looks like she needs to run off a little energy."

And he needed some time alone with Megan.

His daughter grinned, exposing the gap where she'd lost another tooth. "Okay."

She scampered away with Daisy at her heels and Megan fell into step with Gage. Her fingers tangled with his and Gage's heart performed a triple beat. Happened. Every. Time.

"You didn't tell her that Daisy is coming home with you?"

"Not yet." Gage veered toward the walking path the church youth group had cleared through the woods as a service project.

"They're perfect for each other. Both of them have a lot of energy, but Jac said that Daisy is a cuddle bug, too." She slanted a look at him. "What did you mean by 'another list'?"

Gage should have known Megan would pick up on that.

"It isn't the first time Ava's made one," he admitted. "I found one in her pocket a few days before we met you."

"Ah." Understanding dawned in Megan's eyes. "She wrote down all the reasons you should get her a dog?"

"Not exactly." Gage lifted her hand and planted a

kiss on the inside of her wrist. Felt her pulse jump and smiled. "It wasn't about dogs at all."

Megan's brows dipped together. "Then why did you make an appointment to see me?"

Confession time.

"Ava wanted a mom…and she wrote down a list of candidates. I happened to find it when I was doing laundry and I—" Panicked. Freaked out. "Thought she needed a distraction."

"You decided to get her a dog instead of a mom?"

When she put it like that…

"I didn't say it was a *great* idea…" And she was laughing at him.

"Gage!"

"My motives might have been a little questionable, but I don't regret it for a moment. That list brought us together."

"But… I wasn't on it."

"After Ava met you, you moved straight to the top."

Megan's lips curved in a smile.

There was a rustling in the underbrush near the path. Baxter's head popped up, followed by a frantic, "No! Come back!"

Megan turned toward the sound. "Ava?"

Tux, another member of the recon group, yipped.

Gage should have known.

"You can come out," he called.

More rustling, the jingle of a collar, and his daughter bounced out from behind a stump, holding a wiggly Daisy in her arms.

"Did you ask her yet?"

Gage winced. "I hadn't gotten that far."

"Ask me what?" Megan's gaze bounced between them and lit on Gage again.

He'd planned to propose on a romantic walk through the woods, but it suddenly seemed fitting that Ava and the dogs, who'd unwittingly played a role in bringing this amazing woman into his life, shared in the moment, too.

Gage reached into his jacket pocket and pulled out a small velvet box.

Megan's heart stalled. She couldn't think. Couldn't speak.

And, for a moment, it didn't look like Gage could, either. But Ava came to his rescue.

"I think you're supposed to be on the ground," she instructed in a whisper.

Megan pressed her hand against her lips as Gage knelt on the trail strewn with scarlet and golden leaves.

"Megan...you inspire me, and you challenge me, and you remind me what's important." He didn't take his eyes off her face. "I love you and I want to spend the rest of my life getting to know you better. Will you marry me?"

"Us," Ava corrected.

"Us," Gage repeated dutifully.

Megan's throat swelled shut again.

"Yes," she managed to say.

Gage slipped the ring on her finger and the emotion shimmering in his eyes brought tears to Megan's, too.

"I think you're supposed to hug now." Ava looked at her dad like he should know these things.

To Ava's obvious delight, he swept both of them into his arms.

"Like this?"

Ava giggled and Megan leaned against him, felt the steady beat of his heart. The heart he'd trusted to her. Just like he had started to trust her with his doubts and hopes and dreams.

Trusted her with Ava, who Megan loved just as deeply as he did.

The ring on her finger meant they were going to be a family and Megan couldn't wait.

She looked up at Gage and smiled.

"Just like this."

* * * * *

Look for Christmas at Spruce Hill Farm,
a full-length Christmas romance
by Kathryn Springer,
on sale October 2024 from Love Inspired Trade!

Dear Reader,

This verse in the book of James is one of my favorites: "Every good gift and every perfect gift is from above…"

Every gift. Perfect and uniquely designed—with each of us in mind, from a Father who loves us. Some gifts, like wildflowers and fireflies, we can hold in our hands. Others change our hearts. Our lives. Gifts like a new start. Friends. And for Megan and Gage and Ava, becoming a family. I loved writing their story because my family is one of the gifts I treasure most. I've also discovered that sometimes the best gifts are the ones we weren't expecting!

If you enjoyed your visit to Pine Bridge, please visit my website at kathrynspringer.com and let me know!

Joy in the journey!
Kathryn